PIG DOG DINER

Kathleen Stockmier

KATHLEEN STOCKMIER

ISBN-13: 978-0-9977939-2-5

ISBN-10: 0997793929

To Barry, my husband of 23 years

and my biggest fan,

who continues to love and

inspire me now from

Heaven above.

1951 – 2017

Contents

Acknowledgments

When I first began writing *Pig Dog Creek*, my intention was to simply write and publish one novel, not a series of books. It was a lifelong dream of mine, and the icing on the cake, so-to-speak, on my writing career that began in the early 1980s.

I am grateful to all the wonderful readers who shared their thoughts and praises with me about *Pig Dog Creek*, and told me they wanted more. Annie Barton fans now want an update on the main character's life and her future plans in Cook, Tennessee. That inspiration spurred me on to write *Pig Dog Diner,* which picks up down the road in 1968, six years after Annie's escape from the clutches of the Barton family.

Once again, Justin Livingston prepared the cover for printing. For *Pig Dog Creek*, he enhanced the drawing by the late artist Ann Pearle. For *Pig Dog Diner*, he created the entire cover.

I would also like to thank my family and friends for their encouragement and support, particularly my two grown children, Lisa Johnson and Brian Johnson, who continue to inspire and bless me daily with their love, and who have put up with my numerous writing projects their entire lives.

My one regret with this novel is not insisting that my late husband, Barry Stockmier, read it while I was writing it. He fought me on that, throwing his hands up and saying he didn't want to read it until it was completely done. Sadly, he passed away before it was finished.

Introduction

A town without a creek is like a human without a digestive system. As its body of water flows across the land, the creek nourishes the soil and plants, and any bad debris in its path is collected and spit out along the way.

On good days when its belly is full and vegetation is plenty, a creek's essence is high, producing energy that empowers the land around it. This overall good feeling is sensed by plant and animal alike, and attracts a following of believers who know deep down inside themselves that nothing on Mother Earth can survive without water, a substance that is vital for all forms of life.

In fact, it is a creek's claim to fame, and one that the residents of Cook know all too well. And they also know that sometimes those bodies of water catch hold of a silent visitor that sprinkles magic along the way.

Annie Barton was a witness to that magic.

In *Pig Dog Creek*, the novel, readers learned that Annie was given to the Barton family by her father who had stolen pecans off the Bartons' property and was facing jail time. Each morning, she escaped her captors and ran to the creek to cleanse her body of the stench from the two Barton men – her arranged husband, Robert, and his stepfather, Daddy Jack. She bore three children from them and was a prisoner and a slave.

The ringmaster of that dysfunctional brood was a disgusting woman named Mama D who allowed it all to happen under her roof. She was also a person who had a lot of secrets.

They all did.

Mama D and her neighbor, Verneice, would later go to prison for a fight that caused the accidental death of Maydell Stokes, Verneice's mother, whose skeleton was found hanging intact from a tree root in the creek.

It was also the creek that empowered Annie by spitting out a book that she found on its bank. It taught her to read and write, and showed her the world through pictures. Armed with confidence and perseverance, she eventually fought her way out of that hellhole with her husband, Robert, and his parents, by escaping one night from the household prison with her three children and running to an abandoned gas station and mart, which she inherited when Robert died.

With the help from friends, she renovated that property and opened Pig Dog Diner, and this is the story of how education can bring confidence, and confidence can bring strength, and strength can give you a life of your own choosing.

1
THE DINER

Annie slowly maneuvered her old Chevy truck through the soft, wet earth on the road leading to Dub's property. It was noon, and the cool drizzly weather sprinkled a fine mist that covered her windshield. She turned the wipers on and saw Dub up ahead walking his milk cow to the barn. The damp atmosphere wasn't good for his nervous Holstein, whose milk production was always low at the changing of the seasons.

Dub gently patted the cow's large body while steering her through the door, and Annie smiled while watching the tenderness he showed the animal. It was what she loved most about him. He never yelled or showed anger in any way, and he had the patience of a saint.

She wondered, though, if his overprotective nature might keep her from climbing a tall, slick ladder today to pick apples on his property.

The familiar sound of her truck's engine produced a wide grin on his face, and goose bumps cropped up on his arms. He turned around, lifted his baseball cap up and began waving it above his head to welcome Annie to his farm. She rolled down her window and waved back. He closed the barn's door and began walking toward her, smiling from ear-to-ear, with a hay stalk peeking out from the corner of his mouth.

"Hey, baby girl!" he said as he approached her vehicle. "Ain't this a nice surprise. Wat'cha doin' out heer?"

Annie turned off the truck's engine, opened the door and stepped down onto the damp dirt. The mist hit her face and she grabbed her straw cowboy hat and gloves off the seat before closing the door. She, too, had a big smile on her face. Dub had that impact on her. His love made her feel good all over.

"Oh, just wondering if I could pick some apples for pies I need to bake," she said, her lips quivering a bit in the cool air. Then she placed her hands on her hips, looked him square in the eyes, and said firmly, "I know it's not the best weather to be picking, but I have a large order from a customer."

Dub took off his cap and scratched his head. "Bet I know why," he said smartly. "Would this have somethang to do with Clyde's retirement?"

"Yep," she replied, excitedly. "Everyone is going to be there. Dora and her sister are planning a big party and have invited people from Cook and Herndon and who knows from where else."

"With a big party like that, y'all might be needin' one of my fat hogs. I can fire up the pit, but I'd need at least 12 hours of roastin' time."

"That's sweet of you, Dub, but I'm sure Dora's kin has the menu all worked out. They asked me to bake four apple pies. Someone else might be bringing the meat. I don't know that for sure, though. I'll ask."

Dub glanced up at the sky and small drops of moisture touched his face. He looked down at Annie with concerned eyes. "Well, I don't think it's right safe for you to pick them apples today, seeing that the weather ain't cooperatin'. You could fall on your keister, and then whut good would that do anybuddy?"

She gazed at him with a blank stare and an open mouth, trying to decide if he was serious or kidding. He laughed, and that irritated her more.

"You look like a fish ready to be hooked," he said, sticking a hooked index finger toward her mouth.

She didn't think that was funny and pushed his hand away, staring straight ahead at the barn.

"Aww, c'mon now," he said, grabbing her arm. "I'm kiddin'. I've got a bushel of red beauties in the barn ready to be peeled and cored. C'mon, I'll show ya."

He tried to put his arms around her, but she wrestled away, so he grabbed her from behind and held her arms still. When he nestled his cold nose against her right ear she could feel and smell his warm breath that was scented slightly with sweet tobacco. He spit the piece of hay from his mouth, turned her around and devoured her lips.

Aroused by his passion, she kissed him back.

"There's my sweet girl," he whispered in her face. "Do you have any other news to share with me?"

Annie knew what he was fishing for – a positive answer to his countless marriage proposals.

She paused a moment and then whispered softly, "Yes."

His body weakened with the kiss and the touch of her wet skin. He lifted her chin up so their eyes could meet. "Okay, whut's it gonna be?"

Annie smiled and said loudly, "Beat you to the barn!" Then she pushed him away and ran to get her apples. He caught up with her just inside the door and pulled her down into a soft pile of hay.

She looked up at him from the barn's floor and smiled. "Now, Dub, I don't have time for this. I gotta …"

"You gotta what? The kids don't get outta school for two more hours."

He was right, but she had to get a pot of stew cooking on the stove at the diner for the evening's supper crowd. "Yeah, you're right, but I have business to take care of at the diner."

He just kept kissing her face and neck and, finally, Annie just pushed him away. "Sorry, Dub, but I really have to go. Please don't be mad."

Dub stood up and dusted the hay off his shirt and jeans, slicked back his damp hair with his left hand and placed his hat atop his head with the other. "Okay, okay. Let me get them apples for you."

Annie watched him walk toward the back of the barn and knew that she had hurt his feelings. Kissing and hugging had been all she was willing to offer him for the past six years, and she knew he needed more. His patience for her was admirable. He would do anything she asked him to do.

After living in a hellhole for years with Robert and Daddy Jack in a subservient environment, bootlicking and cowering, and being treated like a sex slave, Annie wasn't interested in being intimate with Dub at first. But his sweetness and romantic feelings for her have been refreshing and joyous. She knew kissing him would lead to something more, but it's all she wants right now.

"Maybe tomorrow," she whispered to herself. "Maybe tomorrow will be different."

While driving back to her restaurant with the bushel of fruit in tow, Annie thought about how much she owed Dub, and how she wouldn't even have Pig Dog Diner if it weren't for him.

After Robert died from an infected boar bite, Dub helped Annie acquire the deed to Tinker's Tow & Garage, which Robert's uncle left to Robert and Annie. But Mama D and Daddy Jack wanted the sole rights to Tinker's and, after Robert's death, they came up with a devious plan involving Dub asking Annie to sign a letter that relinquished her rights to the property.

Instead, Dub told Annie about her in-laws' plan and she and her three children, Dwayne, Will and Becky, escaped the Barton house one night and fled to the garage to live.

That was six years ago, and Annie remembers it all like it was yesterday. She remodeled the property and turned Tinker's into a restaurant called "Pig Dog Diner," and upgraded the gas pump outside to industry standards. Against her wishes, Dub started paying rent to Annie for the use of her two-stall garage for his ambulance and wrecker service. Because it was serving the community of Cook, she felt like the space should be rent-free. Dub disagreed and was firm about paying.

The bedroom off the Mart of the gas station was converted to a full-scale kitchen. The adjacent bathroom was remodeled, and an office and storage room was added on to the back of the station. Annie and the kids – Dwayne, 10, Will, 9, and almost 7-year-old Becky – live in Mama D's old house, which Annie inherited when Daddy Jack died from hanging himself from the huge oak tree by the creek where Maydell Stokes' body was found.

While Mama D and Verneice Stokes were in prison for their roles in Maydell's death, their homes went into foreclosure and Annie bought both of them. She rents Verneice's former house to a nice couple from Memphis who use it as a summer home or whenever they want to escape the rat race of the big city. Annie remodeled Mama D's house by adding a bathroom with a toilet and tub, wall-to-wall carpet, new appliances, a new heater and window air conditioners.

Annie's life now has order, stability, respect and healthy children who love Dub like a daddy. And she loves him, too, but with troubled feelings. How can she marry a man when she has feelings for someone else? How can she truly devote herself to Dub when her heart and dreams are filled with another's words and touch?

She still smells Dr. Jonathan Shea's cologne. On warm days when the windows are open, it wafts through the house and almost chokes her. Sometimes it wakes her up at night, usually during a full moon. With the room lit up like a stage, the shadows of the windy trees outside dance on her walls and curtains, hypnotizing her in some way, because the next thing she knows it's morning, the smell is gone, and her bones ache with emptiness.

He's also with her at work. Every time she turns on the radio in the diner it seems like Herb Alpert's No. 1 song, *This Guy's in Love With You*, is always playing. She imagines Dr. Shea singing the lyrics: *"Tell me now, is it so? Don't let me be the last to know … I need your love, I want your love … say you're in love and you'll be my girl. If not, I'll just die."*

The words weaken her resolve until she almost faints; yet, she wishes she had the record to play over and over and over, because thinking about the handsome doctor keeps her moving forward and fills her with hope for the future.

Sometimes the feeling reminds her of the abused Annie six years earlier who used to bathe in the creek every morning to wash the stench of Daddy Jack or Robert from her body. The song's lyrics remind her of how far she's come and how close she is to being like the woman she saw on a torn-out page of a movie star magazine that was blowing along the creek's bank. It was a black and white picture of a blonde lady in a beautiful white dress dancing with a man in a black suit. They were both smiling, happy to be alive and, at the time, Annie imagined their life filled with nice words, pretty music, a white two-story house and a big fancy car.

That dream is closer to being a reality now and she's not giving up on someday making it happen. She is a successful businesswoman who is financially stable. She might drive an old Chevrolet truck, but she can afford a new car. And she knows she is smart and pretty. It's the man that's missing from her vision.

Annie believes that Jonathan Shea *is* that man in the black suit. It has been six years since she has seen him in person, yet her pulse races and tears flow with yearning every time she thinks of the handsome doctor who left Herndon General Hospital to start a private practice in California and marry a woman he believed to be his perfect mate.

"He'll be back," she said aloud while peeling the apples for the pie. "I know he loves me."

2
DR. SHEA

Closing time is the second worst time of the day for Dr. Jonathan Shea. It means leaving his job on the outskirts of Herndon and driving past the exit to Cook – again – in order to reach his home on Lake Wheatley.

Since relocating there from California three years earlier to work at the reactivated Herndon Army Air Base, he has had to fight the urge to visit Annie. Every day he secretly wishes that someone from that little town of Cook would come onto the base and recognize him and tell her he is there.

But in three years, no one has come.

At first, it was embarrassing to be back in Tennessee, so he kept a low profile. Wounded from a toxic marriage that cost him his medical practice, he had to accept what he could not change, rebuild his life and career, and seek therapy. The Army base was a perfect place to start anew and heal.

In the divorce, his former wife almost sent him to the poor house after lying in court about his so-called infidelities and physical abuse. He admitted to being blindsided in the beginning by her beauty and brains, but was completely in the dark about her ability as an actress, which won favor with the jury when she produced crocodile tears and shrieks of heartache that were worthy of an Academy Award.

He had no inkling about her past four marriages or that she had a reputation as a gold digger. In the beginning, he actually thought they were made for each other! With both of them tied to the medical field as physicians, he believed they would travel the world and help people who were living in unfavorable circumstances and conditions.

In the end, he lost more than money, possessions and reputation. He lost his pride.

Thanks to his connections at Herndon General Hospital, he was able to apply at the Army Air Base and was accepted immediately. He enjoys his work with the young men at the military entrance-processing center who have been drafted or enlisted on their own. It is there that Dr. Shea and other medical personnel decide if a recruit is fit for duty. If he is deemed healthy after a battery of tests and inoculations, the recruit is authorized for basic training or boot camp.

While his work with these fine young soldiers is fulfilling, he yearns for intimacy with a woman, particularly Annie. He toys with the idea of them being together, and then tears down the whole idea when he realizes that she does not fit in his world. Or does she? He asks that question to himself on countless occasions. He has read books about love, watched movies about love, listened to dissertations about love, and even visited a psychiatrist about love.

"It's a feeling," one of his doctor friends told him. "You'll know when she's the right one when you can't stop thinking about her no matter how hard you try. If she is the right one, no others will give you the endorphin rush like she does. It's a euphoric high that you've never felt before. It's like a fix a druggie feels when he shoots up, like a dream that allows you to soar like a bird above the clouds and not be afraid of falling. It awakens your senses. It's magical, like your favorite piano concerto that never ends day after day after day."

"It's Annie," he whispered aloud while driving past the Cook exit. "But maybe it was *me* that didn't fit in her world!"

He saw a turnaround in the road up ahead and instinctively pulled off and turned the Army Jeep around to drive back to the exit. It was almost dark and he thought no one would recognize him in the vehicle. He grabbed a green cap from the backseat and put it on his head just in case the Jeep drew attention his way.

His already racing heart began to pick up pace and felt like it was going to burst through his skin. He drove slowly down the two-lane, tarred road leading to Cook and soon caught sight of the outdoor lights on Clyde's Grocery Store. He turned right on a side street between the store and the schoolhouse that he remembered leading to Annie's house and saw even more lights and lots of cars parked near a building.

He stopped in front of the structure that looked like it used to be a gas station. There was a gas pump outside and two garage doors attached to the building, which looked vaguely familiar to him. The lighted sign atop the building said, "Pig Dog Diner." Through the large paned windows, he could see about 20 people sitting at tables eating and drinking. He watched them for a good two minutes, enjoying the sight of Cook's residents socializing over food in a restaurant atmosphere that didn't exist the last time he was there. He was happy to witness the entrepreneurship and progress of the small town.

Then, suddenly, he grabbed his heart and almost wet himself when he spotted Annie walking through the crowd of patrons with a coffee pot in her hand. He watched her work the room like a professional, pouring coffee, engaging in conversations, patting people on the back and hugging customers as they exited. He was mesmerized by her beauty and confidence. He tried to recall how old she was now. Maybe 23?

The last time he saw her was six years earlier in her hospital room at Herndon General. It was during his last week as a doctor there, and she was admitted with a head injury after fainting and falling onto the concrete floor of Tinker's Town & Garage. That was the day they said their goodbyes, and it was a conversation that was tough to get through.

His head throbbed just thinking about those words and high emotions. "She was so young!" he said aloud, beating the steering wheel of the Jeep with both hands. "And it happened so fast! Why didn't I say something? Why didn't I do more to protect her?"

He recalled driving to Cook on the afternoon that she was released because he was having second thoughts about going to California. He wanted to see if she thought the two of them could have a future together if he stayed, but no one answered the door at the Barton home. He believed that no one answering the door was God's way of letting him know it was not meant to be.

"If only someone would have just opened the door!" he cried.

He continued to watch Annie through the window from the

seclusion of the Jeep until a car drove up and honked for him to move. He hated taking his eyes off her. She was more beautiful than he remembered.

Reluctantly, he turned the Jeep around and headed back toward the road out of Cook, a road he could barely see in the dark with eyes filled with tears.

After driving about half a mile, he had to pull over onto the road's shoulder so he could collect himself before continuing his journey to Lake Wheatley.

3
THE MONSTER GODS

Annie sat on the bank of Pig Dog Creek and sipped her hot tea. The kids were due home from school at two-thirty and she was waiting for them to arrive. From two-thirty to four o'clock every day, she and her three children spend time together before she has to leave and prepare food for her customers at the diner.

Sometimes the kids go to the diner and watch TV in her office while she and her hired cook, Henry, prepare the meals. Then they eat there and a babysitter takes them home and puts them to bed. But today, they are eating at home because it's Friday, and that's fried fish night at Pig Dog Diner, and she can't worry about them being there. People will be lining up at the doors right at five o'clock, and the last one will leave about nine or ten. No matter how well prepared she is for fried fish night, she always runs out of coleslaw. But never can she run out of hush puppies. That would be the end of the day, period. Not even banana pudding can save the day when the hush puppies hush.

While sipping her tea, her eyes scan the creek. She is in awe of nature's beauty in her presence. The glistening water of the creek and the abundance of wildlife surrounding it astonish her.

The terrain has changed significantly since she first laid eyes on it when she was 12 years old. At first it was subtle, then it seemed suffocating. But now it is beautiful again with the invasive kudzu plant wrapping itself around trees, bushes, boulders and rusted power equipment, and transforming the land into colossal topiaries that resemble giant bears, elephants, deer, rabbits and other animals.

She calls them her Monster Gods, and her favorite green-leafed beast is the large dog topiary located directly across the creek from where she sits each morning. It reminds her of Rusty, an old hound dog they used to have, who ate something bad, died suddenly and was buried along the creek's bank. Sometimes she thinks she sees Rusty running in and out of the kudzu, but there are a lot of mutts in Cook that look like him.

The water is quiet now. With the fast-growing Japanese vines taking over the banks of the creek, there is a sense of calm and tranquility that wasn't there before the tuberous plant arrived.

And her mind is clear and purposeful now, too. She understands that there is a deep and serious bond between her and Pig Dog Creek, one that she is still trying to grasp. Believing it to be spiritual, she is torn between thinking it is God or her mother. It doesn't really matter. She continues to have nightmares about the vision she saw in the water six years earlier when a mushroom-like stalk topped with large fluffy clouds rose up as high as the trees right before her eyes. In that billowing crown of marshmallow fluff, Annie saw Maydell Stokes' eyes. It was just one of the ways the beloved schoolteacher was trying to unveil her place of death, and also who was responsible.

No one in Cook knows that she saw the stalk. But Annie thought that once Maydell's bones were removed from the creek and put to rest in a cemetery and those responsible for her death – Mama D and Verneice Stokes – were punished, life would get back to normal. Annie would like to think that those days of seeing visions are over, but sometimes there's restlessness inside her body that tells her differently.

She didn't visit the creek for the longest time after Maydell's funeral because she and the kids were kicked out of Mama D's and Daddy Jack's house right after Robert died. They were forced to live in a small room in the back of Tinker's Tow & Garage, which she inherited, and the small living quarters just kept getting smaller as her children grew older.

Right before Annie began converting Tinker's into a restaurant, she and her children moved back into Mama D's house near Pig Dog Creek, which she bought in foreclosure. Daddy Jack's suicide made that transaction even easier for Annie, who suffered at the hands of both of them.

Annie sipped the last drop of tea from her cup and could hear Becky's giggles behind her. They got louder and louder until she could hear her breathing, too. Then two, cool baby-girl hands covered her eyes.

"Guess who, Mama!" she said panting.

Annie smiled and pretended she didn't know who it was. "How many guesses do I get?" she asked, trying not to laugh out loud.

Becky knelt down on the cool earth, but continued to hold her hands like a mask around Annie's eyes. "You just get one, Mama."

Annie put her teacup down and tried to contain herself. "Oh, so I am your Mama, am I? Well, let's see, is it Will? Have you disguised your voice in some way, Will? Because you sound a whole lot like your sister. What's her name?

Becky giggled and pulled her hands off Annie's eyes. She threw her arms around her mother from behind her and smothered her right cheek with kisses. "No, Mama, it ain't Will. Guess again."

Annie grabbed Becky's hands and put them to her lips, kissing the little girl's fingers over and over.

"You sure do taste good," she said. "You taste like Becky!"

Becky giggled and fell into Annie's lap, stretching out across her mother's body and staring at the creek. That's when they both saw a man with a camera taking pictures on the other side of the water.

"Who is that, Mama?" Becky asked.

Annie stared at the young man who looked to be about 20 years old. He was taking pictures of the creek and the kudzu plants that covered the bank. He saw Becky and Annie across the water and pointed his camera at them and snapped a picture. He was tall and thin, blond-headed and fair-skinned, with a cowlick on the right side of his hairline that made his hair stick up like a bird had just swooped down and pecked at it.

He took the camera away from his face and stared at Annie. She recognized the cowlick instantly.

"Noble," Annie said softly, tears streaming down both cheeks.

She reached into her bra and pulled out a handkerchief that she always kept there in case she needed it to wipe her eyes or blow her nose. The hankie is just one of the many survival habits she continues to use from her days in captivity with Robert and his parents. She dabbed her eyes and looked again across the creek for her brother.

He was gone.

Becky noticed her mother's tears. "Do you know him, Mama?"

Annie thought a moment before she answered. Was this the time to tell her daughter that her mother has eight brothers that live up in the hills? And those eight brothers are her uncles? And that she hasn't spoken to any of them since she was sold to Mama D and Daddy Jack when she was just 12?

No, it was not the time or place to lay that on a first-grader, she decided.

"No, hon, I don't know him. He just looks like someone I knew once. C'mon. Let's go find Will and Dwayne."

4
THE TWISTER

The sound of the school bell ringing at 2 a.m. startled Annie from her sleep. It meant only one of two things: a tornado or a fire.

She sprung from the bed, pulled back the curtains and raised the window. The night was pitch black and the wind was blowing furiously, whistling as it pushed its strength through areas not equipped for such power. Limbs from the huge tree out front dropped like toothpicks.

The phone rang and Annie rushed to the hallway to answer it. All three kids were up and clinging to her body.

"Hello," said Annie.

"Annie, it's Dub. Thar's a tornado outside of Herndon headed our way. I'm a'comin' to git you and the kids. Git dressed. See you in five minutes." Then he hung up.

Annie was stunned. She looked at the phone, looked down at her crying kids and listened to the bell ringing. Then she snapped to. "Quick, kids! Put some warm clothes on – and your shoes! Dub's coming to get us in five minutes!"

All of them started crying. "What's the matter, Mama? Is it a hurricane?" asked Dwayne. He had studied them in school recently and knew their strength.

"No, baby, it might be a tornado," Annie replied as calmly as she could. "We have to get somewhere safe, like a basement. Mr. Dub is going to help us, so don't worry, okay? Just get dressed."

They were tying their shoes when Dub reached the front porch and began banging on the door. He carried Becky in his arms and set her on the backseat of the truck. Then he went inside for the boys, who were standing at the door holding hands and ready to walk out into the storm. Once he got all three in the truck, he put blankets around each one. They were afraid and shaking. Annie jumped into the front seat and Dub ran around to the driver's side and got behind the wheel. He reached over and grabbed Annie behind the neck and pulled her mouth to meet his and kissed her. "We're goin' to be alright, baby girl," he whispered in her face. "Everyone is goin' to the church's basement, but there ain't enough room for the whole town, so we're goin' to Martha Wilks' house. She's got a root cellar."

Martha lived not even a quarter mile away, yet it seemed like the longest ride of Annie's life. She saw the school's playground equipment topple over and sparks were flying from power lines along the road that looked like massive doses of fireflies. All types of debris – signs, house siding, wood posts, newspapers and even clothing – was blowing around, with some items landing on Dub's windshield, causing him to act quickly by rolling down his window and sticking his arm out to pull the clutter off the glass so he could see to drive his precious cargo to safety.

Dub drove the truck alongside Martha's house where the root cellar was located. Annie jumped out and grabbed Becky. Dub lifted Dwayne and Will from the truck and told them to hold hands and run to the cellar doors that were wide open and waiting for them. Once inside, he quickly chained the two wooden doors together. Several people, including Martha, were sitting on overturned buckets with their flashlights beaming. The cellar was cold, smelled like mold, and had a dirt floor, but Annie knew they were safer there than in her house. The kids were shaking, but not crying. They were tough kids.

They huddled together in a corner and covered themselves with their blankets, asking Jesus to watch over them and protect those who were in harm's way. They could hear things hitting the door, windows breaking in the house above them, and the wind howling as it made its way through Cook. Then, all of a sudden, it was quiet. Dead still. Dwayne smiled and looked at his mother. She raised her eyes and smiled back, but then frowned when hail began to pelt the cellar doors and house. It felt like they were all in a cardboard box and someone was throwing huge rocks at it.

Not long after that began, maybe three minutes, they heard a train driving through the house above, and then a huge tremor, like an earthquake, shook the root cellar's floor. They held each other tightly while waiting for something to blow up. But, instead, it started to rain.

"I think we're okay," said Dub. "I think it blowed over."

Someone's transistor radio that had gone to static was now operable. An announcer's voice was coming in loud and clear. "Once again, we need to remind folks not to touch any wiring that is on the ground. There are a lot of live wires across Herndon and its surrounding cities. We are receiving reports from unnamed sources that say that half of Cook is gone. I repeat. Half of Cook was in the path. If you have loved ones living on the eastern portion of Cook, pray that they had a basement or cellar, because there are no structures standing in that part of the town."

Annie began to cry and reached out to Dub. She could hardly talk. "Dub … would you say that my house … is my house on the eastern side? Or not?"

Dub hesitated and thought for a second before answering. "I think y'all are on the edge, that's for sure. But don't be gettin' upset 'til we can see for ourselves at daybreak, okay?"

Annie nodded.

Dub patted her hand. "Look at it this way, hon. We're okay, right? We can rebuild anythang. *Anythang.*"

"What about your farm, Uncle Dub?" asked Dwayne.

Dub thought about the farm he almost bought on the east side of town and was so happy to hear the west side was spared. "Ahh, it's prob'ly safe. I don't think it was in the path, but I bet thar's a lot of work that has to be done 'cuz of high winds and such."

They huddled together the best they could until daybreak broke through a teeny crack between the root cellar's thick wood doors. Dub couldn't wait to get outside and look at the damage. He thanked Mrs. Wilks for allowing them to take shelter there, and he rounded up Annie and the kids to leave. He walked up three of the six steps leading out of the cellar, unchained the two wood doors from the inside, and threw them open. Cool air began circulating inside. He could see white clouds and blue sky from the middle step and smiled. Then he reached the top of the stairs and fell back, grabbing the doors' frames to steady his body. When he pulled his body up and out of the cellar, the devastation was overwhelming. He closed his eyes and counted to ten because it usually worked to regain his bearings sometimes when he thought he was going to faint. After a few seconds, he opened his eyes and saw that his truck was gone, and so were all the houses on the street. He turned around to see a slab of cement where the Wilks' home once stood and fell to the ground sobbing. He managed to motion to Annie with his hand to stay put. All he could think about was his ambulance in the garage at Annie's restaurant. If someone could get him there, he could drive a lot of people to the hospital. Then he had a sinking feeling that maybe it would be gone, too.

Survivors were walking around like zombies, wondering what they were going to do now and where they were going to go. It was eight o'clock in the morning and no one had arrived yet to help. Then he spotted Clyde. He waved his hands high up in the air and Clyde maneuvered his truck through the debris-laden road to reach him.

Clyde jumped from the truck and ran to embrace Dub. "Man, I am so happy to see you, Dub!" he said joyously, patting Dub's back. "Is Annie and the kids with you?"

Dub nodded. "Yeah, they are here and jest fine."

"Well, let's grab 'em up and get 'em home. Our part of town is still in one piece."

Overjoyed, Dub began to sob. He bent over and put a hand on each of his knees and let out a big cry. Clyde patted his back and Dub's sobs eased. He stood up and looked into Clyde's eyes. "Can you git us home?" he asked. "Then I can git the ambulance. You know there are gonna be riders."

Clyde walked back to the root cellar with Dub to help Annie and the boys walk over to his truck through all the wreckage on the ground. They all began to cry when they saw the houses gone, the trees uprooted and the roads buckled. They knew they were the lucky ones. All Annie could think about was checking on Henry and his family and seeing if he could come to the diner and cook some food for all the displaced people. Her mind was going a mile a minute thinking about all the things her little community needed.

"Now, Annie," Clyde said, "don't be thinking that you gotta save the world, because I know how you are. You're thinking about feeding and clothing and taking care of families and finding them shelter. And that's all good. But we have the Army Corps of Engineers coming to clean up debris, provide emergency housing and construct public facilities. So you'll have some help with that."

Annie just sat motionless, except for her shaking hands. "You mean from the Army Base outside Herndon?"

"Naw, these will be national guys coming in, but I bet our local Army will get involved in some way."

"Well, then I'd better get cooking," she said.

5
THE CREEK

The tornado had a mind of its own, some said. Its path of destruction was unlike any they'd ever seen or heard about. It traveled up on a northern path from Herndon and hit the eastern part of Cook with a vengeance. Most of the residents who lived on the east side of town were from the farming community and had underground root cellars to get into for protection. But many didn't know it was coming and were blown away while they were asleep in their beds.

The death toll at morning's light was 23, with 20 unaccounted for.

The monster force of wind spawned several smaller tornadoes, and one cut a path along the inside of the creek.

"That's just the damnedest thang I've ev'r seen," said Sheriff Larry Haynes, while surveying the ruination of Pig Dog Creek. "It jest locked itself into the creek's path and rode it out to the end like a bucking bronc. I ain't ev'r seen a tornado do that. They *always* jump the creek."

Elwood Jones spoke up. "But we're not talkin' 'bout a normal creek here, Sheriff," he said. "Remember when we spotted Maydell's bones holding onto a tree root inside that crick?"

"Yeah, yore right," he replied. "This heer ain't no normal body of water."

The offshoot tornado dug a path along the winding creek and added at least two more feet of depth to it. Rubbish and fragments of life that were once whole and useful were scattered along the bank – bike rims, tires, bottles, clothing, broken dishes, tin cans, animal carcasses, broken boards, aluminum siding, a baby stroller and more decorated Pig Dog's bank at every turn. It was like the body of water threw up its contents and spewed them out along the top for everyone to see. The only water in Pig Dog now was from the rain.

The tears that flowed that day after the storm could have filled that creek back up to its normal height. Broken, bewildered, confused and in shock, the residents of Cook took comfort from their caring community members and went through the motions of picking up the pieces.

Crops were ruined. Acreage that was flourishing with fall vegetables now stood in deep water. Most of the pecan trees down in The Bottoms that were flush with nuts were naked in their orchards, stripped of the product that many of the farmers depended on for income. The Baptist Church was gone, but most of its parishioners made it to the basement and survived. And they were not alone in their grief. Herndon residents were grieving, too.

In addition to the flooded croplands, communities within 10 miles of the Mississippi River, like Cook, were told to be prepared for flood issues that might be headed their way.

The U.S. Army Corps of Engineers' emergency response team was on its way to help provide disaster relief to the flood victims and to support recovery operations in the wake of the disaster. Help from Memphis was coming in the form of volunteers and supplies, too. Everyone was stepping up to help, even if it was just holding someone in their arms while they cried.

Annie's house was untouched. The small tornado that cut a path down the creek didn't even loosen a shingle on her structure. The windows were all intact, the swing was blowing in the breeze on the porch, and the trees were standing firm and unscathed. Her eyes filled with tears when she spotted all the trash on the creek's bank. It looked like Uncle Deek's still and junkyard had relocated there. The barn was gone, but it was on its last leg anyway. She hated that nasty barn and all the wasps that set up their nests in the corners of its roof. That dark, stinking place with a door was one of Daddy Jack's secret spots to have his way with Annie. She should have had it demolished a long time ago.

"Thank you, God, for the safety of my family and loved ones, and for our house not being blown away," she said looking up to Heaven from the front porch of her home. "Please give me the strength now to help others repair their lives."

Pig Dog Diner suffered a few broken windows, loose and missing roof shingles, wet floors and a power outage. But between her and Dub and the kids, everything got cleaned up quickly and the electricity was restored, too.

Dwayne, Will and Becky put fresh cloths on the tables and took orders from the customers. No one was going to be charged for food, so the children didn't have to handle money. Their mother was busy frying up hamburgers, French fries, bacon and onion rings. Clyde came by with more groceries – macaroni, cheese, Yoo-hoo chocolate drinks, bread, rag bologna, Coca-Colas, cookies and pies.

"Let me know if you need anything else," he said while putting everything in the diner's kitchen cupboards and fridge. "My nephew, Marty, is driving up now from Memphis and relocating here. He's one of those guys that can do anything, you know? Like fixing a car or a radio or a television set. He is strong and can move furniture. I bet he can fix that old freezer of yours."

"Oh, that would be a blessing, wouldn't it?" she said, big-eyed. "It will be nice to have your nephew here, Clyde. Sorry we have to put your retirement party on hold."

Clyde readjusted his baseball cap and looked at her with sincere eyes. "You know, Annie girl, I don't think I'm ready to retire yet."

She wasn't ready for him to retire either. "Good! Then that's settled!" she said. "Thank you so much for all the groceries."

He turned to leave, but then stopped. His eyes were wet with tears. "You know how proud I am of you, right?" he asked.

She wrapped her arms round his large torso and planted her head on his chest. "Yes, I know, Clyde." Then she raised her head up and looked into his face. "Remember when I first came into your store?"

Clyde laughed. "Yeah, you were a sweetheart. You didn't know what to do first, how to pay or what anything was used for."

"I know. I was a mess," she replied, her cheeks flushing with embarrassment.

"And look at you now," he said, wrapping both arms around her. "I couldn't be more proud of the woman and mother you have become."

Her tears dampened Clyde's shirt. She withdrew from their embrace and looked up into his eyes. "Thank you, Clyde. Thank you so much for helping me and guiding me."

"It was my pleasure, Mis' Annie. I'd better get back to the store now. I'll check on you later." He started walking toward the door and then turned around suddenly. "Oh, I almost forgot," he said. "I'll bring Marty by for dinner."

Annie smiled. "I can't wait to meet him," she said sweetly, returning to her stove and all the greasy food awaiting her. The kids were in her office watching television and listening for the door's bell to ring with customers. They jumped up and ran to the eating area when they heard it go off when Clyde entered, and were disappointed when they saw him because they knew he wasn't staying to eat.

Annie left the stove for a minute to blow her nose in the bathroom when she heard the bell ring again. *Oh, wonder what Clyde forgot now?* she thought.

She heard the kids' feet run past her door in a hurry and the next thing she heard were their screeches of delight. "Must be Dub," she mumbled to herself.

She washed her hands and was wiping them on her apron when she approached the door into the diner, expecting to find a hungry Dub wanting her to cook him his favorite meal of hamburger and fries.

"Mama, Mama, look who's here!" shouted Will with a sucker in his hand.

Annie stood in the doorway of the diner and saw Dr. Jonathan Shea kneeling down with Will's arms around his neck and Dwayne and Becky hugging him from behind.

Her mouth dropped and her eyes rolled into the back of her head. She started to fall and Dr. Shea stood up and caught her before she hit the floor. He cradled her head in his left hand and brushed back the hair from her face with the other hand. A tear from his eye hit her cheek and, like on cue, her eyes opened slowly.

She looked up into Dr. Shea's eyes and forgot how to speak. She stumbled for words. "Am . . . I . . . dreaming?" she whispered hoarsely.

He caressed her cheek with his hand, and his hypnotic cologne made her even more light-headed.

"No, you're not dreaming, Annie. It's me," he said softly.

At that very moment, like clockwork or divine intervention or a supernatural occurrence, Herb Alpert's No. 1 song was playing on the radio. The familiar words and music made her smile.

"Let me help you up," he said, clutching her under each arm and pulling her to her feet. He put his arms around her shoulders and she shuffled to a table and sat down.

The kids caressed Annie's arms and planted kisses on her cheeks while she sat at the table. She asked them if they'd like to walk over to Clyde's for an ice cream while she talked to Dr. Shea, and they screamed with joy. Annie reached into her apron's pocket for the money, but Dr. Shea put up his hand to stop her.

"My treat," he said, reaching for his wallet in the back pocket of his pants. He gave each one of Annie's children a dollar bill. Their mouths dropped and their eyes widened at the sight of the paper money.

"Don't spend all of that on ice cream and candy," Annie said. "Save some for another time."

"Okay, Mama!" Dwayne yelled as they ran out the door.

Annie looked around the diner and no one was sitting at a table, but it was almost time for a suppertime crowd and she knew her talk with Dr. Shea was going to be interrupted soon with customers. She looked at him and smiled.

"What are you doing here?" she asked, nonchalantly.

He reached across the table and grabbed her trembling hands. "Seeing how you're doing," he answered.

His touch generated a multitude of goose bumps on her arms. She looked at his hands and noticed he wasn't wearing a wedding band. She struggled to get her words out. "So … um … why … are you . . . um … here … and not with your wife somewhere saving lives?"

He put his head down and took a deep breath and then looked back up into her eyes with a serious face. "Well, you're not going to believe this, but she was not the person I thought she was, and we are divorced."

Annie tried to hold back a smirk and other exciting jitters she had floating in her veins. She put her hand over her mouth for a second to get a grip on her emotions and then removed it. "So, are you back in Herndon at the hospital?" she asked casually.

"No, I'm working at the Army base. I've been there three years now."

She gritted her teeth and tried to think clearly. *Three years?* she thought. *Three years? All this time he's been just a few miles from me and he hasn't even bothered to see how I'm doing?*

She didn't know what to say next. She just stared out the window with a blank face.

He reached over and touched her chin and pulled her face toward his. Their eyes met again. "I know what you're thinking," he said softly. "It took me a long time to get my head on straight after the divorce. She took me to the cleaners, threatened my life, destroyed my credibility and ruined my career. I was not a whole man when I got the job at the base. I am in a better place now."

His words made Annie feel sickish. She wasn't a whole person once, either, and could identify with his pain. She was all too familiar with people making you feel worthless. Somehow his dilemma caused her suppressed feelings of imprisonment in the Bartons' house to surface. Her heart and mind were racing, but she managed to speak.

"I am so sorry that happened to you," she said sincerely. And with a boldness that came out of nowhere, she asked, "So what does that mean for us, exactly? Does it mean that we can see each other now?"

His face flushed red. Surprised by her self-confidence, he quickly replied, "Yes, if you would like that. It's all I have thought about for three years."

Annie gazed out the window of the diner and hesitated for a moment before she responded. She had dreamed of this day for *six* years and now, here it was. *He expects me to just say okay and forgive him for dumping me for another woman? Why does he love me now? Where was that love six years ago when I was going through pure hell and living in a run-down gas station?*

She turned to face him and he was staring a hole through her. She smiled and reached out for his hand and held it tightly. "I think we definitely have a connection," she said confidently, "but I am an old-fashioned girl and need to be courted. So, yes, I would like that."

He pulled her hand up to his lips and kissed it. It smelled like bacon grease. "Mmmmm... have you been cooking bacon or is this your usual smell?" he said, jokingly.

She yanked her hand from his. "Yes. A bacon burger. It's our house specialty. Want one?" she asked, in a conceited, yet silly way.

"I'll take four. How do your kids like them cooked?"

6
THE INJURED

Dub asked his cousin, Owen, to help out with the wrecker service while he drove the ambulance to and from the Herndon hospital with Cook's injured residents.

It had been a very, very long day of digging people out from the rubble of destroyed homes. The sounds of voices calling for help beneath a pile of wood, sheet rock or twisted furniture and appliances was joyous sometimes, and horrific at other times after assessing their wounds.

The hardest for Dub and other residents who helped was the discovery of babies and small children who had perished under the weight of their collapsing structures. None of the parents who survived would let Dub take their deceased children without them along, and more times than not, that road to Herndon was filled with a wailing mother and father cradling their dead child or children.

On the way back from Herndon after a trip with grieving parents, Dub had to pull off on the side of the road and cry it out. He thought about Annie and how lucky she was to have her three children who were not harmed by the stupid monster tornado. He thought about what it would be like to pull little Becky's lifeless body from a pile of rubbish, and he cried even harder. He couldn't wait to see her and the rest of Annie's family and hold them tight. He loved them more than he had ever loved anyone or anything in his life.

He decided that after his last run to Herndon, he'd stop by the diner and check on Annie and the kids. He needed something to eat, too. On the tarred road back to Cook, he saw someone up ahead waving their arms to flag him down. As he got closer, he recognized Ethelyn Gibbs. He pulled over and rolled down his window.

"Lawdy, Mistah Dub," she said, panting, "Percy done sent word 'bout Cal in The Bottoms. He ain't good."

"I'm real sorry to hear that, Mis' Ethelyn. Hop in. I'll getcha there."

Ethelyn could hardly walk around the vehicle to get in on the other side. Dub had never seen her that weak in his whole life. She had nursing skills passed down to her from generations of midwives, and she had probably been busy all day tending to the injured black community of Cook. And now it was her son, Cal, who needed her.

She walked around to the other side of the ambulance and saw that there was no backseat. Dub noticed her dismay and reached over and opened the passenger side of the vehicle. She stuck her head in and began sobbing louder.

"Don't worry about what other people think, Mis' Ethelyn. Please get in and let's go get Cal, okay?"

"Yessir," she whispered. Then she slouched down in the passenger seat and covered her head with a sweater.

Dub just let her be. He was more worried about the rickety bridge they had to go across to reach The Bottoms where Cal was working. It might not have survived the winds, he thought. And, if it had survived, the weight of the ambulance might cause it to collapse.

About a quarter-mile before the bridge, he spotted the surviving workers walking toward them on the road. Two men were helping Cal walk. His leg was bleeding, sliced open by a piece of flying aluminum. They carried him to the ambulance and Ethelyn climbed in the back with him. She started talking to him, telling him everything was going to be all right, that she was going to sew up his wound and nurse him back to health. Dub turned on his emergency siren and drove them back to their home, which, remarkably, was still in tact.

It was dark now and he was beat. He heard on his two-way radio that the American Red Cross was in the area and hoped that many of Cook's residents were able to get some help from them. Lots of strange vehicles were on the roads around Cook, and he knew they were all trying to help in some way.

He could hardly wait to see Annie and the kids and chow down on a burger. He pulled into Pig Dog Diner's parking lot and saw Annie through the windows working the crowded room with a coffee pot in one hand and a platter of food in the other. She was all smiles – considering the kind of day it was for everyone – but a smile can be like a ray of sunshine for many searching for hope.

Annie's kids were worn out and sitting at a table near the door waiting for someone to take them home. When Dub walked in, they ran to him. He broke down in tears.

Dwayne, the sensitive sibling of Annie's three children, was concerned. "What's the matter, Mister Dub? Why are you crying? Has it been a bad day for you?"

Dub could hardly talk. "Yep, you could say that, young man. But now I am crying tears of joy for y'all. I love y'all so much!"

The kids just held onto him tighter. "We love you, too, Mister Dub," said Becky.

Will was quiet. "Whut's up, big guy?" Dub asked him. "Why you so quiet?"

"I got a sucker today," he said. "Do you have one for me?"

"No, son, I sure don't," Dub said. "Next time, okay? What color do you like and I'll buy some from Clyde. They will be great to have in my ambulance for some of the children I meet."

"I like red. Like the one the doctor gave me," Will said.

Dub looked up at Annie, who was within earshot. His heart was beating so loud and fast that he thought he was going to have a heart attack. He tried to talk, but he couldn't catch his breath and fell back into a chair. She put down the coffee pot and rushed to his side.

He looked up at her with a blank stare and searched her face for a sign of hope. She pushed his hair off his brow and wiped his face with a white washcloth from her pocket.

"Now, Dub, it ain't what you think," said Annie. "The doctor did come by today to see if we were okay, but that's all."

Confused, Dub's face wrinkled up. "What? He was jest in the neighborhood? Why is he here?"

Annie held his face in her hands and kissed his cheek. "He works at the Army base, Dub. He has worked there for three years. He was just checking on us."

Dub's breathing calmed down. His heart was almost beating normal but his mind was still going strong. *Three years, huh? And this is the first we've heard of him? Guess he's over her*, he thought. *Or he would've been here sooner.*

7
THE MISSING

After the tornado struck, the weather was cooler. The humidity disappeared and any leaves that were left on the trees began turning to fall colors. Hearts still ached with the loss of human lives, crops, livestock, houses, possessions and dwellings. But Cook's sense of community was more alive than ever.

Annie's daily routine was starting to come back around, except for her morning ritual of visiting the creek. It just didn't seem as important anymore, especially since all the critters, leafage and water had been blown away and debris still lingered on its bank.

But one morning while washing dishes, she was overcome with an urgency to visit Pig Dog Creek. Trancelike, she picked up her hot tea and grabbed a sweater from a rusted nail on the back porch and started walking toward it. The morning light was bright enough for her to see clearly because the clocks weren't going to change for another month. She approached the bank with caution, aware that the clutter the tornado unearthed from the creek's bowels was splattered everywhere.

Annie smiled when she saw a spot near her favorite tree that was dry and free of litter. She eyed a large log nearby and placed it up against the oak to sit on. The creek was in shambles. The green kudzu that had wrapped itself around the trees lining the creek and created huge animal topiaries in the process was gone. She could see right through the tornado-ravaged oaks, ash and sycamores, which now stood like giant toothpicks on the other side of the creek, picked clean of their leaves, bark and animal inhabitants. Instead, an old house, barely standing on its foundation, was visible through the ravaged thick. Her mind went in all directions at the sight of that dwelling. She thought about all the mornings she was naked and bathing in the creek, and how someone could have been watching her from the other side. Or how she could have been raped or kidnapped, and how Robert, his parents and her children would have never known what happened to her.

Over the past six years since being on her own and opening the diner, her visits to the creek have not been an everyday occurrence. But she has never forgotten the power and mystical forces that lie in its viscera, now visible before her, deplete of its internal parts.

The calmness she once felt for the creek was gone, just like the critters, the topiaries and the cool water. Instead, a sense of urgency to get back to the house took over her emotions. She poured the tea out on the ground and took one last look at the place she used to confide in – the place that knew all her secrets and her desires and taught her how to read and write with the help from a book it coughed up on the bank.

"I will miss you, my friend," she said, sobbing. As she turned to leave, something began glowing brightly from a pile of regurgitated crud about 10 feet away. She looked all around to see if anyone was watching, and slowly walked toward the glow. With each step, its glow dimmed slightly. While standing over it, the glow diminished completely, and she reached down and picked up the object. It was a metal box with a padlock on it, probably swallowed and submerged years ago by the creek and thrown up on the bank just recently by the tornado.

Annie knew this time that the box had a really good chance of being just that – a box. Nothing else. No magic or ghost of someone's dead mother teaching her to read and, consequently, uncovering a homicide.

"People find things along the creek all the time," she said aloud, while walking back to the house.

She opened the back door to the porch to place the box on a shelf and was met by Dwayne and Will.

"Ain't Becky with you, Mama?" asked Will.

"No, hon, she wasn't up yet. I was by myself," she replied.

"Well," said Dwayne, scratching his head, "She ain't in her room."

"Did y'all look in the bathroom?" she asked.

The boys nodded.

"How about out front?"

"Yep," they replied.

Annie tore through the house like a wild woman, looking in every closet, under every bed, in the bushes alongside the house, under the house and in the well. Exhausted and crying uncontrollably, she called Dub on the phone for help. He called Sheriff Haynes.

Everyone in Cook knew something was wrong at Annie's house. Dub had an early morning call to Herndon General Hospital with a customer and was on his way back when he received a message on his Citizens Band radio that Becky was missing. He turned on his truck's siren so he could get there faster, and so did the sheriff. Some people thought the sirens were warning them about another tornado coming, and many of them ran out of their homes to see what was going on.

Thank goodness for a calm Sheriff Haynes, because no one else could talk as plain and unruffled as him during a catastrophe and get others to cooperate. He sat everyone down in the living room and told them to be still and listen.

"Mis' Annie, when was the last time you and your youngins saw Becky?" he asked.

Immediately the boys yelled out in unison, "Last night!"

"Now, boys," the sheriff said politely, "I know you want to be good helpers, but let your mother reply, okay?"

The boys nodded their heads.

Annie blew her nose and looked up at the sheriff with swollen red eyes. "It was last night, sheriff, when I put her to bed."

"Was everything okay with the two of you? Was there a disagreement or bad words between y'all? Did you notice that anything was bothering her?" he asked.

"No, sir. She was just her perfect little self," she said through her sobs. "We talked about going to the creek this morning, and that it was about time we paid it a visit … you don't think she went to the creek, do you?"

Dub burst through the front door and looked like a wild man. His hair was uncombed, his red eyes were opened wide and wet, and he talked loudly. He knew by the look on everyone's face that Becky was still missing.

"Is she still gone?" he screamed.

Annie got up and ran into his arms. The boys hugged his legs.

Dub caressed Annie's head and patted the boys that were affixed to his lower torso. "What do you think, Larry? Maybe she just got up and wandered outside? Maybe fell back asleep somewhere?"

Annie began to wail. "Oh, Lord, please don't let my baby be taken by a stranger!"

"Now, now, Mis' Annie," the sheriff said. "I've seen cases like this before where the child is simply asleep in a vehicle or outside with a toy or followed a dog somewhere and got lost. Does she have a favorite doll? Because she may have taken it with her. If that's the case, she could have left by herself and taken her doll for company."

Annie ran to search her room and came back empty-handed. "No doll. That's good, right? That she has her doll? That means she is just out for a walk somewhere."

"Let's hope so," Mis' Annie," he said. "We'll get a posse of volunteers together and comb the area."

The doorbell rang and six women from the church were standing on

Annie's porch with covered bowls of food. They came in and headed for the kitchen to put away the vittles before returning to console Annie.

"Now, Mis' Annie," said Martha Wilks, "you know we'll find her. She's just wandered off and fallen asleep. You'll see," she said, patting her back. "You'll see. It's just a matter of time before she'll walk through that door."

Annie buried her head in her hands and sobbed loudly. She raised her head when she heard male voices talking outside. She got up to get some fresh air and saw her front yard and back yard crowded with men looking for Becky. A light went off in her head and she ran back inside to tell the sheriff.

"Sheriff Haynes!" she screamed, pushing everyone aside to reach him in the kitchen before he left to round up the men and execute a search plan. "I just thought of something."

The sheriff turned around. "Everything you give us is important," he said. "What is it?"

"This morning when I went out to the creek, I could see a house on the other side," she said, panting. "It was an old house, but I didn't even know it was there. But the trees are bare now and I could see it. Could you check that house? And see who owns it?"

Sheriff Haynes said he would. "But you know the likelihood of her being acrost the crick is slim. No little girl would even try to crawl over all that muck and wade through more mud and then climb back up the other side. But we'll look. You just keep thinkin' about other places she could be, okay?"

Dub held her tightly. "Yessir," Annie said trembling. One of the ladies went to the other room to get Annie a warmer sweater to put around her shivering body.

Dub walked Annie over to the couch and the ladies went into the kitchen to make coffee and breakfast for everyone. He told her he didn't want to leave, but he wanted to be a part of the search team.

"No, go ahead and go," said Annie. "I will feel better knowing you are out there doing something more important than holding my hand. You have good instincts and I know you'll find her."

He kissed her forehead and walked toward the front door. "Don't worry, hon. We'll find her."

Annie just wailed louder.

Dub stopped at the door and looked back at her. She looked up at him through tears.

"I love you, Annie Louise," he said, all choked up.

Annie smiled and nodded her head. "I love you, too, Dub."

It was the first time in Annie's life that she had said those words to an adult other than her mother.

"He's a good man, that Dub, ain't he?" said Martha, rubbing Annie's back.

"Yes, ma'am, he is," replied Annie.

"Let's go in yonder and get you a cup of hot coffee and something in your stomach," suggested Martha.

Annie thought a cup of hot coffee would probably keep her from shaking and being so cold, so she agreed. She sat down in the kitchen facing the back porch's window and saw Sheriff Haynes' cowboy hat coming up the back steps. She was lifeless as she watched him enter the back porch and then open the door to the kitchen.

In his hand was Becky's doll. Annie fainted and fell to the floor.

8
THE BRIDGE

The doll was lying in plain sight in a bush across the creek, like someone had thrown it there. Lem Smithers' son, Tim, grabbed a vine embedded in the creek's wall and climbed up to retrieve it. Sheriff Haynes let the dogs get a good whiff of it before he took it into the house.

The posse of men continued to scour the creek. Half of them took the east side and the others headed west. Each group of volunteers had a trained hunting dog. All of the search team had grown up in Cook and knew the creek better than anyone. But the creek before them now was unrecognizable. Lem and Tim brought their two 'coon dogs. Ike Burns brought his bloodhounds, and Andy Drummond brought his beagle, Blue. The dogs were skittish, retreating at times for no reason and then plowing forward at other times and coming up empty.

There wasn't a lot of creek left on the east end of the creek because that portion of Cook was hit the hardest by the tornado. Its dirt walls had collapsed and stopped them from searching there. That's when they realized that one of those small, offshoot tornadoes must have begun its journey there and headed west.

On the west side, the trees were bare and the creek was dry, providing a path to travel. They peeked inside the windows of the old white house that Annie told them about, but no one was inside. Searchers entered the front door and walked around inside, but found nothing. No sign of life or trap doors or anyone living there for years and years.

They continued west and were joined by the rest of the posse who had reached a dead end on the eastside. The dogs were barking and running up and down the creek, jumping over downed trees, dead branches and brush and moving forward. Then there was silence. The men looked at each other with concerned faces and cocked their rifles. They trudged through the creek's soggy bottom as fast as they could to reach the dogs and were taken by surprise at what they saw.

Before them was a wooden bridge over the creek that connected the two banks.

Lem took off his cap and wiped his brow with a handkerchief from his back pocket. With a baffled look on his face, he said, "Did y'all know 'bout this?"

"Naw," said Ike. "Whar you think it goes?"

Sheriff Haynes caught up with them as they were staring at the bridge. "Well, I'll be gall damned!" he said. "Who in the hell has balls that big to build this heer bridge without lettin' anybody know?"

Andy piped up with a smirk on his face. "Maybe it's some sorta outer space place like from the *Twilight Zone* or somethin'."

Lem nudged him in the back with a stick. "Yore not right in the head, kid. Ain't no alien shit. C'mon. Let's get up thar."

The dogs had no problem climbing the creek to reach the top. The men, however, weren't in shape and found it difficult to scale the sludge. They grabbed the embedded roots sticking through the muddy walls of the creek to reach the top. Tired and out of breath, they walked slowly across the unstable bridge, thinking any minute that it would collapse with their weight. They reached the other side and looked for the dogs. They were nowhere in sight.

Andy blew his dog whistle, but Blue didn't come. His mind was going a mile a minute with all kinds of ideas about why Blue wasn't coming.

"He always comes!" he cried. "He ALWAYS comes! Maybe they killed him! Maybe they kill animals along the crick and eat 'em for supper!"

"Shhh!" said Lem. "Listen."

The men stood still and heard someone talking. The sheriff motioned for them to start walking slowly in the direction of the voice. The closer they got, the more they could understand what the person was saying. And then they heard Becky laughing.

All of the men's mouths dropped and their eyes widened at the sound of Becky's laugh. They almost cried from happiness. But who was she with? Why did they take her? Sheriff Haynes pulled out his revolver and started walking ahead of everyone toward the voices. He stopped and turned back around toward the men.

"Stay here," he told them, quietly. "*Stay here.* If I whistle, then come get me."

Bravely, Sheriff Haynes continued to walk forward. During his 13 years as sheriff of Cook, he had never had a child go missing or a tornado kill half of his town. He just didn't know how much he could take, but he knew one thing: he was taking that little girl home to her mama.

He stood behind a tree and watched the young man and Becky. The man had a knife in his hand and a piece of what looked like wood in the palm of his other hand. The sheriff watched him as he whittled the wood, blowing it off every now and then and then whittling again. Becky watched him intensely, clapping her hands when he stopped, jumping up and down with excitement, and laughing at the funny faces he was making.

Finally, the man put the knife down and stood up. When he did, Sheriff Haynes was ready to move in. But then he stopped suddenly when he saw the man hand the little wooden doll to Becky.

"What's her name? What's her name?" Becky asked, jumping up and down with excitement.

The young man put his index finger up to his mouth. "Shhhhhh!" he mouthed.

Becky quieted.

"It's Ida May," he said, as he handed the carved figure to Becky.

Becky kissed the doll and put it over her heart. "I love you, Ida May," she said.

Sheriff Haynes started walking toward the young man, startling him. He stood up and raised his hands high. Becky ran to the sheriff and said, "Look what I got! Look what I got!"

The sheriff looked down for a second at Becky and the young man ran off into the woods. He pointed the gun to shoot, but had second thoughts. He'd find him somehow, he thought. He'd arrest him for kidnapping. But he doesn't deserve to be shot.

Then he scooped up Becky into his arms and walked back toward the men waiting for him. The dogs came running toward him from the thick of the woods and everyone was happy.

"I've gotta git you back to yore mama, Becky," he said to the little girl. "How come you run off like that and worry your mother?"

Becky put her head on the sheriff's shoulder. She started to pout a little and then hugged his neck and whispered in his ear.

"He said he was my uncle," she said softly. Then her face wrinkled up and tears flowed down her cheeks. "He said he loved me."

9
THE SEARCH

Dub was wondering when an opportunity would present itself so he could investigate the creek on the eastern side of town without looking suspicious. Becky's disappearance gave him the perfect occasion to do so.

The east side of the creek was impassable for water, human or beast, thanks to the recent tornado. However, the bank was the most likely place to find what he was looking for: a locked box that he buried behind the Wilks' property a few months earlier. He waited for the volunteers to finish their search for Becky there before he conducted his own.

Everyone in Cook had their own means of protecting their valuables because the bank vaults were located in Herndon, about 30 minutes away. Living in the country afforded its citizens many creative places to hide their cash or other valuable belongings. Some put money in socks and stuffed them in mattresses. Others filled empty jars or tin boxes and buried them in the yard. He even heard of one family putting their jewelry in a pail and dropping it down into the dried up well and placing the lid over the top.

Dub was worried. Maybe the tornado had dredged up his box. Or maybe it hadn't. He didn't know anything for sure, except the likelihood of someone finding a metal box with a padlock, buried about three feet deep in the creek behind the Wilks' home, was possible. He knew that now. It was proven six years ago when torrential rains dredged up a human skeleton belonging to Maydell Stokes that was buried there during a drought.

He scoured the east side banks of what was once the creek and came up empty-handed, so he decided to return to Annie's to see if Becky had been found. He pulled up to her house in his truck and saw lots of people sitting on the porch and standing in the yard. He caught sight of Becky on the porch's swing in Annie's arms and was relieved. Will and Dwayne ran to greet him. He rolled down his truck's window.

"Where you been?" asked Dwayne.

"Looking for your sister. I see she's back," he said from the inside of his truck. He opened the door and Becky jumped out of her mother's arms and ran to him.

"Hey, baby girl!" he said, scooping up her tiny body into his arms. "You had us so worried."

Becky looked him in the face and said, "Where were you, Mr. Dub?"

Dub thought for a moment and said, "I was looking for you, hon, on the other side of the creek. I couldn't find you, but I knew someone would."

He put her down and she ran to her mother. Annie began walking toward Dub with a face that could kill.

"What's wrong?" he asked her.

Annie thought a minute before she replied. "What the hell do you think is wrong?" she replied. "All this time I thought you were out there looking for my baby and you were off in your truck somewhere! Where'd you go?"

"I was looking for her," he said calmly. "I was at the eastern part of the creek. I really didn't think she had wandered over there, but I wanted to be sure. Who found her? Where was she?"

"There's no eastern part of the creek anymore, Dub," she said sarcastically.

"I know that, Annie. But it's an area where she could have wandered and gotten hurt. Someone had to check it out."

"There was a posse that went that way," she replied coldly. "And they searched that part. They said it was closed off. There isn't even a creek over there anymore. It's all filled up with dirt and debris. Why would Becky be over there in a place that is so uninviting?"

Sheriff Haynes overheard their conversation and got up from his seat on the porch and began walking toward the couple.

"Annie, Dub, I'm headin' back to my office to take care of business," he said loudly.

Annie threw her arms around the sheriff. "I can't thank you enough, Larry, for all you did today for my family," she said sincerely.

"Well, it ain't over yet," he replied in her ear while patting her back. "We've got to find your bother and see what's going on there. I'll be talking to you tomorrow to see where he lives. Up in the hills, you say?"

She and the sheriff were looking eye-to-eye now. "Yes, way, way up in the hills."

Dub was dumbfounded. "Your brother?" he asked. "Your brother kidnapped Becky? Who is your brother?"

"You know I have eight brothers, Dub. I think it was the oldest, Noble. Becky and I saw him a week or so ago across the creek taking pictures. I am pretty sure it was him."

"And we ain't sure it's kidnapping," said the sheriff. "He didn't mean her no harm. I witnessed that myself. But he did look like maybe he wasn't right in the head."

Annie began sobbing. She put her hands over her face and ran into the house. Everyone who was sitting or standing around her property got up and walked to their vehicles.

Dub followed her inside and caught up with her in the kitchen. "Is there anything I can do for you, hon?" he asked.

Annie thought for a moment. "Yes," she replied sternly. "You can leave."

Dub was stunned, like someone had just shot an arrow through his heart but he was still able to breathe, but just slightly. "Okay," he said softly, and walked toward the front door with his head hanging low.

Annie walked to Becky's room and told her it was time for her bath.

She turned on the tub's water and started helping her sweet girl get undressed. Mud was everywhere – her clothes, shoes, fingernails and feet. She piled the clothes onto a large towel and carried it to the washing machine on the back porch. The sun was going down and the insects outside were calling for their mates. She poured the detergent into the machine and began walking into the house when she thought she saw someone in the yard through the screened porch window.

"Who's there? she asked, through the screened door.

There was no reply, just silence. Even the bugs hushed.

"Noble? Is that you, Noble? If so, please come here to me. I won't hurt you."

She waited about a minute before he emerged from behind the tree. She opened the door slowly. He was about three feet from the steps leading up to the back porch. He stopped, looked up into his sister's eyes and said, "I'm sorry, Sis. I jest wanted to tawk to her."

Annie reached her hand out to him and he flinched backward. "No!" he said. "Don't touch me!"

"Okay, okay ..." she whispered. "Would you like to come inside?"

"Naw. I have to go."

"Will you come back? Because I'd like to get to know you again," she pleaded.

"Naw. Not a good idee."

"Okay ... okay. Whenever you're ready to talk I am here for you," she said calmly. She turned to go back into the house and then decided to take one last look at him.

Noble was at the end of the yard now. He saw her standing there and cupped his hands around his mouth and yelled, "I love you, Annie Louise. I love you!"

Annie dropped to the floor sobbing. "I love you, too," she answered hoarsely with tears running down her cheeks and splattering on the linoleum floor.

"I love you, too."

10
THE CUSTOMER

Annie arrived at the diner earlier than usual because her neighbor and babysitter, Lindy Sue, had spent the night, allowing her to leave the house early before the kids got up.

Every day the brunette teenager catches a bus at eight o'clock in the morning in order to reach the high school in Herndon by 8:45 a.m. That works perfectly for Annie's family because the elementary school in Cook starts its day at eight.

In fact, the bus to Herndon Memorial High School picks up its passengers from the elementary school's parking lot, so having Lindy Sue as a sitter works well for everyone. At the end of the day, Dwayne walks his brother and sister over to the diner for an after-school snack, and then he walks them home. If it's raining, Annie or her cook, Henry, drives them home.

Henry is Clyde's nephew. He is 35 years old but acts more

like he's 50. The confirmed bachelor is an old soul who lives on the outskirts of Cook with his mother, Eula, who is Clyde's sister, in an area known as The Bottoms.

The Bottoms is a low-lying area of Cook that always swells with water when it rains. The only crops that really flourish down there are orchards of pecan trees, and every one of them belong to Annie. She bought the land from Mama D's estate when it went into foreclosure, just like she did with Mama D's house and Verneice Stokes' home, too. Annie worries about Henry every day because he has to drive across a rickety old bridge above The Bottoms that isn't fit for cars, trucks or school buses. Every now and then Annie will have a dream about the bridge collapsing and a busload of kids falling into the muddy pecan groves below, and police and firemen pulling their bodies up one by one.

Henry has a lot of connections in town because his family has roots in Cook and Herndon dating back to the mid-1800s. Several rows of the orchard that survived the tornado's winds look promising for harvesting, but three-quarters of the trees were stripped bare in the storm. Henry has hired workers to collect all the fruit on the ground to determine if the nuts are too wet and have started to rot. He pays them per pound, and Annie and Henry also pay the workers to shell a good portion to sell in the diner and Clyde's store. She freezes a lot for the spring months of cooking. All of the pecans will fall over the next 30 days or by the end of November.

Annie's walk to the diner from her house takes about three minutes by foot. In the dead of winter when there's snow and ice on the ground, she drives her old Chevy truck. But today's fall morning is cool and breezy, perfect walking weather for her. As she approached the diner, she was surprised to find a customer waiting outside on the bench. An Army Jeep was in the parking area and she wondered who was hovering near the door at six-thirty in the morning.

She was almost afraid to approach the person for fear of coming face-to-face with a looter or vagrant, but was pleasantly surprised to see Jonathan Shea's face shining in the moon's light. For just a split second, her mind traveled back to her early moonlit mornings in Pig Dog Creek after a successful escape from the Barton house, those mornings when the oaks swayed their branches like arms waving 'hello' to her, and when she dreamed of being in the arms of a handsome man.

And there he was.

"Hello, there," she said quietly, as if she was afraid to be heard by anyone other than him.

"Hello, again, Annie," he replied. "I pass your exit every day on my way to and from the base, and today I decided to stop by to see how you are doing and grab a cup of coffee and a cinnamon roll."

Annie's whole body lit up like a Christmas tree. Tingles were crawling down her legs and up her arms, on her neck and between her legs. She could hardly talk for breathing so hard, and it was difficult to mask her excitement upon seeing him.

He sensed that excitement like a well-trained bird dog on a

rabbit, scooping her up and holding her close. She smelled his familiar cologne on his neck and nearly fainted with joy. Then he found her mouth and pushed his tongue inside. Never had she felt such a wonderful thing inside her body in her entire life. So this is what sex is all about, she thought, because that's what she wanted right then, and so did he.

There they were in front of her diner's door acting like two animals in heat and she didn't care. Except people were starting to drive by on their way to work and she knew she had to open the diner or take him around back and forget all about feeding anyone in town. She grabbed his face with both hands and said, "Right now I want you more than anything, but I have to open this diner before I become the talk of the town and have to wear a letter H on my chest."

He pulled back and looked at her face. "So you've read *The Scarlett Letter?* Consider me impressed! What does H stand for?"

She felt her face blushing, but laughed anyway. "Hussy!" she said. "Yes, I have changed a lot since our first meeting. I couldn't even write my own name when I first met you. C'mon in and let me get you some coffee."

Her hands were shaking and she had difficulty getting the key in the lock. He put his hands over hers and guided the key inside the carved hole. It opened and she flicked on the lights. They were both blinded for a second, but recovered quickly. She scurried to the kitchen to put on a pot of coffee. He took off his jacket and placed it on a coat rack and settled into a booth near the window. It wasn't long before they could smell the coffee brewing. She walked over to his booth and sat across from him. He was the first to speak.

"I was relieved to hear that you were okay after the tornado hit. I spent that night at the base because the weather was so bad. I was asleep in a cot in the infirmary when Clyde called. I figured you asked him to call me, right?"

"Yes. I wanted you to know right away that we were all fine," she replied.

He reached across the table for her hand when lights from a customer's car lit up the diner.

"Duty calls," he said, sadly.

"Yes, sorry," she said frowning. "I was thinking that maybe you could come by the house after work and have dinner with us. The kids would love to see you, and I'll have Henry take care of things here at the diner."

The bells on the door chimed as three men entered. "I'll get your coffee and cinnamon roll and then see you tonight?"

A big smile broke out on his face. "I can't wait."

He scooted out of the booth and grabbed his coat off the rack. Annie was scurrying around with a coffee pot and filling cups. She could still sense Jonathan's presence in the room and wanted to just drop everything and run into his arms, get into his Jeep and spend the rest of her life with him.

She motioned for him to wait and he stood patiently by

the door. She slipped a cinnamon roll into a bag with a napkin and poured a cup of coffee into a paper cup.

"Is black coffee okay? Or do you need cream and sugar?" she asked sweetly.

The grin on his face was from ear-to-ear. "No need for the sugar," he whispered. "I got enough from your lips."

Annie blushed with excitement.

"Thank you, Mis' Annie, for the grub," he said loudly for the other patrons to hear.

She tried not to laugh at his attempt to talk like a local because it would have offended her customers, so she just smiled and said, "My pleasure, Doctor Shea. You come back now, ya hear?"

"Yes, ma'am," he replied with a big grin.

She watched his Jeep back up and drive away. Daylight was now taking over the sky and, again, her thoughts were transported back in time to her morning bathing ritual in the creek when she was a prisoner in the Barton home. She recalled a recurring daydream during that time of being swept across a curtained room by a handsome man wearing a tuxedo like the one she had seen on a page torn from a movie star magazine that was blowing along the creek. The man in the picture was dancing with a woman in a white flowing dress, and she imagined him stopping every now and then to whisper in her ear, "I love you, Annie Louise."

And she had imagined looking into his blue eyes and smiling back, almost fainting with excitement.

I am that woman now, she thought, as she walked around the diner refilling her customers' coffee cups.

Dreams really do come true.

11
DUB'S MISERY

No one had seen Dub in a week. He couldn't be contacted by CB radio or telephone. No one had seen hide nor hair of him since Becky went missing.

Tongues were waggin' around Cook that he was licking the wounds that Annie inflicted on him when he failed to join up with the search team that was looking for her daughter.

"Surely he knew that my harsh words were coming from a mother whose daughter was missing," she said to Clyde one day in the grocery store.

Clyde knew about Dub's disappearing ways, but it had been a while. "Don't worry, Mis' Annie," Clyde said, "he'll resurface soon. He ain't done this in quite a few years, but sometimes he drops outta sight and jest needs time to get his act together."

Annie had not seen that side of Dub, nor had Dub seen that side of her when she verbally blasted him on the day Becky went missing. She could always count on Dub, but on the *one day* that she needed him more than *anything*, he was not even a part of the recovery crew of volunteers like he said he would be.

She knew she was the reason that Dub was AWOL. Her words stung her mouth and spit fire on him when she told him to leave after Becky had been found. His disappearance made her realize how much she really didn't know about him.

"Where is his family?" Annie asked Clyde. "Does he have parents or brothers or sisters somewhere?"

Clyde motioned for his helper to take over the cash register and he walked with Annie out to the front porch of his store. The men who played dominoes on the porch every day had gone home, and it was a pleasant place to sit with a cool breeze that didn't require a coat.

"I will tell you what I know," said Clyde, "but it ain't pretty, I can tell you that. Do you still want to know?"

Annie thought for a minute. She stared at Clyde's two-story, white house next door and knew that he and his kinfolk had lived in that very same house for over a hundred years. She knew she was talking to a man of his word, and a good, decent man she secretly wished was her father. Then her mind wandered to her flesh-and-blood daddy who was a no-good scoundrel and cheat. A man who gave his only daughter to a family of heathens because he didn't want to go to jail for stealing pecans on their land. Her heart started beating fast.

"Yes," said Annie. "I want to know. I can handle whatever you throw at me."

"Okay, then," said Clyde, with a serious face. "I'll tell you, but you didn't hear it from me, ya hear?"

Annie nodded yes. "I understand."

Clyde took a puff off his pipe and the sweet aroma was soothing and hypnotic for Annie. "Dub was found in an abandoned box car over in Herndon alongside the tracks that run north and south."

Annie gasped. "How old was he?"

Clyde took another puff and just let the words flow from his mouth. "He was eight years old. Mighta been ten. No one really knows. Anyway, he hadn't had a bath in God knows when. He told everyone he taught himself to hunt and ate a lot of wild game. A panhandler taught him how to build a fire and steal things during the night from people's porches and kitchens. The Herndon police locked him up overnight, but he got out some way. Pete Bilbow found him the next morning in one of his tow trucks, and Dub talked his way into a part-time job cleaning Pete's vehicles and keeping his garage clean."

Tears flowed down Annie's cheeks as Clyde continued telling her about Dub's early years. She felt worse now for talking to Dub in such a hateful way.

Clyde looked into her eyes. "I can stop now, if you like,"

he said.

Annie thought for a minute and realized there was never going to be another talk like this again, and she'd rather hear it all now. "No, sir, please continue."

"Well, he grew up in that there garage and learned the towing business. Pete bought a cot and put him up in a room off the shop. There was a bathroom next to it and he cleaned up there. He paid him some wages, but not much. What he earned he spent on food and that was all. The rest he saved to buy his own truck."

Annie blew her nose and Clyde stopped. "I told you it was a tough story to tell," he said, "but you and Dub ain't that far apart in your struggles to survive."

She had no idea. Here she thought she had the worst story to tell anyone about her life, and then Clyde tells her this doozy about Dub. "Does Dub know anything about his parents?" she asked.

"Oh, yeah," he answered. "That's how he got the farm."

Annie's jaw dropped. "What?"

"Yeah, his ma and pa had sex and she got pregnant. They had to get rid of their son so they could inherit that property, so they took their baby over to a brothel outside of Herndon and left him on the porch."

Annie was puzzled. "I don't understand. Why couldn't they keep the baby and the property, too?"

Clyde had sweat on his brow even though the outside temperature on the porch was in the low 60s. He drew in a deep breath and coughed. He took a handkerchief from his front pants pocket, wiped his forehead, and looked away from Annie when he said, "Because his ma and pa were sister and brother."

Annie stood up quickly and her face broke out into a fierce crying spell. She wailed like a child into her cupped hands and Clyde got up from his chair to comfort her. He held her on the store's porch while she cried it out.

"I know it's a lot to swallow," said Clyde, patting Annie's back. "But it is something that this young man lives with on a daily basis. That's why his heart was so open to you and your kids. He knows what it's like to be unwanted."

Annie raised her head from Clyde's massive chest. "I guess what I don't understand is why they got rid of the child. Was that in the will? Did his mother and father have to get rid of their baby in order to keep the farm? Did his grandparents know that Dub was a product of incest? Oh, my stars! I can hardly say that word with Dub's name all over it now!"

"I don't rightly know," said Clyde. "I can only speculate on this, but I believe Dub's grandparents knew they were both dying and wanted their two children to have the property and keep it in the family. They didn't know about their daughter's pregnancy. She hid it from her parents somehow. We don't know anything for sure, but giving that baby to the brothel may be the reason they both committed suicide later on down the line, and they left the farm to Dub as repentance of their sin."

Annie heard all she wanted to hear for now. It was all so heartbreaking. She wanted to see Dub in the worst way. She left Clyde's porch and began walking over to the diner when she spotted Dub's wrecker backing out of the diner's garage. He pulled up next to her and reached over to roll down the window on the passenger side. The door was unlocked and she jumped into the front seat and right into his arms.

"What's the matter, baby girl? Did someone die while I was gone? Are the kids okay? Are you okay?"

He listened to her sob a few minutes and then she sat upright in the seat. "Dub Thomas, don't ever leave and not tell us where you are going, do you hear me?"

A big smile broke out on his face. "Let me guess," he said. "You missed me, right?"

She beat his chest softly with both fists. "Yes!" she cried. "We all missed you. I don't know how we could ever live without you."

Annie put her arms around his neck and they just sat there in the road for about five minutes holding each other. Dub was loving every minute of this time with Annie.

"So, Mis' Annie, does this mean you'll marry me?"

She squirmed in the seat a little and sat up and looked him right in the face. "I can say, Mr. Dub Thomas, that it is something to be considered."

Then he leaned forward and kissed her mouth, and she

kissed back.

"Don't ever leave like that again, you hear?" she asked.

Dub closed his eyes and savored the moment. "Yes, I hear," he whispered.

12
THE UNINVITED DINER

Annie and her three children were sitting near the front of Pastor Russell's makeshift church inside the elementary school's cafeteria when he called her name. She had been thinking about Jonathan Shea and wasn't listening to his sermon. She just looked at him with a surprised expression.

He repeated his request from the lectern. "Annie Barton, would you please come up here?"

Surprised and flushed, she rose slowly and turned around. Everyone was smiling, like they knew what the pastor was going to say. Annie's mind was reeling with guilt and she thought she might pee her pants. She took slow and cautious steps toward the pastor while mentally preparing herself for humiliation. She thought he knew she was in love with two men and he was going to tell everyone that she was going to burn in Hell unless she repented for her sins.

He turned her around to face the congregation and she prepared herself for the slurs that would be spit on her. She stood before them like a mummy while he walked behind her and grabbed each of her hands and held them above her head.

Everyone's eyes were on her, and Dwayne, Will and Becky started whimpering. Then the congregation stood up and began clapping.

"These are the hands that helped heal a community," the pastor yelled from behind Annie.

"Amen!" the congregation yelled back.

"These are the hands that cooked for the hungry and the homeless, the emergency crews, the displaced and the downtrodden, the forlorn and forgotten, and the strangers at her door."

"Amen!" they shouted back.

The pastor let down her hands and placed his own hands on her shoulders, turning her body toward his. He looked into her eyes and said, "Thank you, Annie Barton, for your selfless gestures, your kind heart, your generosity and delicious food you prepared while our town was reeling from the worst tragedy in its existence. God's light is shining on you today, Annie."

And, just like that, the clouds outside gave way to a ray of light that burst into the school's cafeteria. Annie began to weep, not because she was moved by the light, but because she did not feel worthy of such adulation and praise.

"Now, now," said Pastor Russell, patting her shoulder. "We hope those are tears of joy." Then he turned to the congregation and yelled loudly, "Because of the extensive damage from the tornado to our community, and because of loss of life and property as a result, I received word yesterday from Sheriff Haynes and Mayor Hicks that we are eligible to obtain federal assistance for our recovery efforts."

Cheers of joy, hugs, praises and shouts of thanks to God rang through the cafeteria.

Annie left in the middle of all the pandemonium and praises and started walking out with her children. On her way to the diner, she began to cry again.

"Whut's wrong, Mama?" said Becky. "Why ain't you happy?"

Annie looked down at her sweet little girl and said, "I am, hon. I am."

"Then why you cryin'?"

Confused and rattled and full of guilt, Annie replied, "I am just not that worthy, hon. There are so many other people who deserved the praise more than me. That's all."

Immediately, Dwayne spoke up. "That's not so, Mama. You are the nicest person in the world."

Tears welled in her eyes and she grabbed her three kids for a group hug. They giggled and started running toward the diner.

"Hey, wait!" she hollered. "What are we going to fix today for all the congregation?"

They stopped and turned around and stared at their mama with questionable faces. Then Dwayne shrugged his shoulders. "It don't matter what you cook, Mama. Everything you make is good."

"I want meatloaf," said Will.

"I want fried chicken," said Becky.

"And what do you want, Dwayne? This is your second chance to say!" asked Annie.

Dwayne thought for a moment, and then replied. "I want chicken pot pie."

"Then that's what it is! Chicken pot pie. That is a lot of work! Do I have any helpers?"

All three kids raised their hands. They ran to the diner and were out of breath when they reached the door. A car was parked in front. No one was in it.

"Hmmmm …" said Annie. "Y'all know whose car this is?"

The kids shook their heads "no."

A dressed-up woman wearing a hat with a veil over her face was holding a leash attached to a small dog and walking toward them from the side of the diner.

"Y'all open now?" she asked sarcastically.

Annie recognized her voice. She did not respond.

Perturbed, the woman spoke louder. "I said … are y'all open now? I've been on the road for hours and I need somethun to eat and drink."

The kids were tugging on Annie's dress. "C'mon, Mama, let's go in," whispered Will.

"Why don't ya listen there to your kin, girl, and open this heer place up now."

Annie put the key in the lock and told the kids to go inside and get the diner ready for customers. Will looked at the fat lady and her little dog and then at his Mama.

"Ain't you comin' inside, Mama?"

"Not just yet," she said. "Scoot along. I'll be there in five minutes."

Reluctantly, Will went inside with Dwayne and Becky, but walked over to the booth near the window and kept his eye on his mother.

"So you're out of prison now, huh? What are you doing here?" Annie asked.

Mama D brushed back the veil from her hat and stared a hole in Annie, but Annie didn't flinch. "I just want some vittles, that's all," she said, putting a cigarette in her mouth and lighting it.

Annie pointed to a sign in the window. "Can you read, Dorthea? I don't remember you ever going to school, so you may not be able to, unless your girlfriends in prison taught you. But that sign right there says I have the right to refuse service to anyone. So get your ratty ass off my property or I will call the law."

Mama D started laughing. "You think yore all high and mighty, don't ya. You always did think you were better than everyone else."

"God will be the judge of us," said Annie. "But I know I haven't ever killed anyone like you have. It's a sin to kill another human being, and it's a sin to treat other people like slaves. It's also a sin to let your husband rape your son's wife. If I was you, I'd be doing a lot of praying to get through those Pearly Gates."

Mama D let out a raucous laugh. "You ain't changed a bit, whore," she said. "I want my house back and a few other things you took of mine or you will regret it."

Annie was so angry she was about to spit nails. She turned slowly, walked into the diner and locked the door behind her. She calmly made her way to the wall phone in the kitchen and dialed the sheriff. She no sooner hung up the phone when his siren was blaring down the road.

Mama D heard the siren and was sitting in her car when the sheriff drove up. He walked over to her car and tapped on the driver's side window with his knuckles. She rolled it down.

"Hello, Dorthea," he said nicely. "I didn't know it was time for you to get out of prison. What can we do for you today?"

Mama D said she didn't know what he could do for her. "It's whut that damned girl needs to do for me."

"And what would that be, Dorthea? Annie doesn't owe you nothin'."

"She damned sure does!" yelled Mama D. "Them kids are my kin and I have rights as their grandma. I got me a lawyer."

Sheriff Haynes had heard accusations like this before from felons who were released from prison. He knew that many of the incarcerated were lawyers or inmates who had worked for lawyers who would promise their fellow convicts anything in exchange for money, cigarettes or sexual favors. Promising them legal help to gain access to their children or grandchildren was an age-old scam.

"Well, good for you, Dorthea," said the sheriff. "Now, according to the proprietor of this establishment, I am ordering you to leave or be incarcerated and your car seized. Your decision."

She let out a hearty laugh and started up her Buick. "Good to see you, Larry," she said sarcastically. "I'll be in touch."

She sped down the road and almost hit Dub's wrecker as he was pulling onto the street. He shouted an obscenity and flipped the driver the bird. Then he saw the sheriff and pulled in next to his vehicle.

"What's goin' on, Larry? Who was that?"

The sheriff took off his hat, wiped his brow with his handkerchief, and put his hat back on his head. "That was Mama D," he said coldly. "And she's out for revenge."

"Does Annie know she was here?"

"Oh, yeah, she knows," said the sheriff. "Mama D had a few choice things to say to her."

"Well, I'll be damned," said Dub. "I thought the old broad would get herself killed in prison and we would never have to see her again."

"Naw, we couldn't get that lucky," said the sheriff. "She'll be back."

13
THE RAPTURE

Annie cleaned up the diner after the last Sunday customer left, said goodbye to Henry, and began locking the door from the outside when car lights hit her back. She turned around and saw Jonathan behind the wheel. She smiled and walked toward him.

"Here, let me help you with that," he said reaching for the huge chicken pot pie that he knew was his dinner. "Sorry I couldn't get here earlier. We are short-handed at the base and many of us are having to work overtime."

Annie was tired and he could see it in her face. Church wore her out emotionally, Mama D gave her a headache, and she was hot from cooking so many dinner pies.

"That's okay," she said. "I couldn't have gotten away from here any earlier than this. Everyone was so excited about the money we are going to get to rebuild our town and they just feel like they are on a good path right now, you know?"

He smiled and kissed her gently on the lips. "Yeah, I know that feeling," he said. "C'mon, I'll drive you home. Who's with the kids?"

"Lindy Sue," she said. "They should just about be ready for bed, but when they see you, it might be nine o'clock before they tucker out."

"That's fine," he said. "I don't have to be at work so early tomorrow because I worked late tonight. So don't worry about me."

She climbed into his Jeep and he reached over and pulled her hair away from her temple so he could plant a kiss there. She closed her eyes, smiled and inhaled his cologne. Goose bumps lifted the hairs on her arms. She was hoping he couldn't see that going on, but he was a doctor and they know all about how the body functions.

The kids were happy to see their "Doctor Shea" when he walked through the door. They had just bathed and were wearing pajamas. Jonathan offered to walk Lindy Sue home, but she said her dad was on his way. He showed up a minute later.

Annie put the pie in the oven to warm a little bit and then joined Jonathan and the kids in the living room. There was no way they were going to bed anytime soon. They were so wired. By eight-thirty, they started to poop out and Jonathan helped her put them down for the night. He had to promise them that he would come back again soon. Everything just seemed so perfect.

Annie and Jonathan sat in the swing on the front porch with a blanket over their lap. She told him about Mama D coming up to the diner and he was surprised at the woman's gall.

"After all that woman did to you? And she wants grandparents rights? Is there such a thing?" he asked.

"Larry says there isn't, and he thinks it's just a way for her to have a leg up, you know? That she has something on me that she's dangling in front of my nose to keep me upset. But my houses and business are all legally sound, so I'm not too worried. I just thought my days with her were over, that's all."

Jonathan looked at her in the moonlight and couldn't contain himself. He pulled her face toward his and kissed her mouth gently. She returned the passion, and in no time they were crawling all over each other in the swing.

"Let's go inside," she whispered in his ear. "Let's do this right."

They got up from the swing and walked through the screen door, turned off the porch light, bolted the front door, turned out the living room lights and went into her bedroom. She walked around the room pulling down the window shades and pushing the floor-length curtains together. Then she turned toward him and brought her sweater up and over her head. He took off his loafers and then his shirt, all the while staring at her breasts bulging in her bra. She couldn't take her eyes off his hairy chest.

At one point, she thought she would faint with ecstasy. Making love was something she had never experienced. Sex was always a brutal and unemotional connection for her with Robert or Daddy Jack. But this was something magical and beautiful. She was empowered.

He stayed the night, but left before the kids got up. She walked around in a cloud all day with his panting sounds still in her ears, and a glow that made her look and feel younger and prettier. Her thoughts were consumed with the handsome doctor – his chest, his hands, his mouth and his manhood. Making love to him allowed her to let go of her past and embrace a new future. She wallowed in the daydream all morning until Dub had to go and ruin it all.

"So, whose Jeep was that at your house all night?" he asked her at the diner the next morning.

Dub's question caught Annie off guard. She had asked Jonathan to move his Jeep under her neighbor's carport because she didn't have a garage where he could park it. If he didn't, everyone in town would know that she had a visitor for the night with his vehicle parked in front of her house. Since her neighbors were in Memphis and Annie owned their house, she felt it was okay to use the carport. Jonathan understood completely and moved his vehicle. But it was no business of Dub's, and she was irritated with him for asking about it.

"What do you mean, Dub? There was no Jeep outside my house."

"There was around nine o'clock last night," he said. "And this morning I saw it leave the carport next door."

Annie was furious! Her heart was pounding and her face began to flush with heat. Was Dub out there all night watching her house?

"Well, then, there you have it!" she blurted out. "You know my neighbors allow their friends to use their house when they are down in Memphis, right?"

"Yeah, but I've seen that Jeep before," he remarked.

"Well, now you've seen it again and it will probably be back. So can you just get over it and have some breakfast?"

"Naw, I'm not hungry," he said. "See ya later."

14
THE HILLS

Sheriff Haynes drove his police car up into the hills of Cook. He had a difficult time driving because the tornado had ripped up the road like a zipper. The right side of his police car hugged the mountainside, but about halfway up, the road was intact and he continued to the Slayton compound … or shack … or railcar … or whatever they lived in up in the hills.

He drove slowly because there were no addresses or mailboxes anywhere like there are in Herndon. Folks in Cook had to get their mail from their post office slot inside Clyde's grocery. Many of the homesteads were back off the road, but he got lucky when he saw a handmade sign nailed to a tree that said 'Slayton,' the family's name. It was at the entrance of a dirt road leading down into the brush. He steered his sedan slowly to avoid holes or sharp debris and came upon a house. Two blond men were sitting on the porch with shotguns across their laps.

The sheriff slowly opened his door and put his hands up in the air. "This here the Slayton home?" he asked.

No one responded.

"I said, 'This here the Slayton home?' "

The young man on the right got up from his chair and cocked his rife. "Who want to know?"

"I am Sheriff Haynes representing the Cook Police Department," he said loudly. "I'm not here to arrest anyone. I just need to talk. That's all. I can leave my weapon in my car."

"No need for that, sheriff," a voice said from inside through the screened door.

The door opened and another Slayton brother walked out onto the porch. "I know who you are, and I know why yore here."

Sheriff Haynes was relieved and let out a big sigh of pent-up air from his lungs. "Where can we talk, son?" he asked.

"See that picknick table over yonder? That do?"

The sheriff looked at it and said, "Yes."

The two men sat on the large, sawed off tree stumps across the table from each other and didn't say a word for about a minute. Then Sheriff Haynes spoke up.

"I recognize you from the creek," he said. "You were with Becky and ...

The young man butted in. "I didn't hurt no girl," he said loudly, ramming his pointed finger on the wooden tabletop. "I ain't no purrvert."

The sheriff took off his hat and wiped the sweat off his forehead. Then he combed his hair with his fingers and put the hat back on. It was a cool October day, but the sun was so gall darn hot, he thought. Maybe it was his nerves.

"I know you aren't, son. I know you know that little Becky is your kin."

His eyes filled with tears and he looked away. The sheriff could see his mouth quivering. Then he turned and looked him straight in the eyes. "I love my sister and I love her kids, but she don't want no part of us, and I don't blame her. Look at us! My daddy would've killed us if we went near her. But he is dead now, so we do what we want."

Sheriff Haynes was moved by Annie's brother's words. "Sorry to hear that your father is gone, son. Are you Noble?" he asked.

"Yessir."

"Where are the rest of your brothers? Ain't there like eight of y'all?"

"Yessir, there was. Just three left." He pointed to his two brothers on the porch and said, "That's Boone on the left and Edward on the right, but we call Edward 'Buddy'."

Sheriff Haynes got up from the table and walked toward

the porch. The boys stood up and leaned their rifles up against the house. The sheriff extended his hand and Boone shook it. "Nice to meet you, Boone," the sheriff said. Then he stuck out his hand for Buddy, but Buddy would not shake the sheriff's hand.

"He don't mean nothin' by that, sheriff," said Noble. "He ain't got two of his fingers, that's all. They wuz cut off in a varmint trap. The other hand is like that, too, but wurse."

Sheriff Haynes felt sickish when Noble told him that it was Buddy's thumbs and little fingers that were cut off both hands. He tried not to vomit, but acid came up into his throat.

The young men on the porch looked to be about 19 and 20. The sheriff knew that Annie was the oldest at 24, so Noble had to be about 22 or 23.

"You the one who was in the military?" the sheriff asked Noble.

"Yessir. I was discharged," he replied.

"Yeah, I know," said the sheriff. "I did a little research on you after Becky went missing. You takin' your medication?"

Noble was surprised that the sheriff knew about his mental illness. "No sir. I don't have no way to get it, and no money either. I'm doin' okay. Really."

Sheriff Haynes shook his head. "If yer sick, son, you need the medicine. And if I tell Annie that I met you, she will want to see you."

Noble got physically upset when the sheriff mentioned his sister's name. He put his head down and started walking in circles and mumbling to himself. "Naw, sheriff, don't tell her where we are. She don't want us and she never came back."

It was clear to Sheriff Haynes that Annie's brothers did not know that their father sold Annie to the Barton family. They did not know that she was a prisoner in the Barton home, raped, and had no way to contact them. Only over the past six years has she been a free woman, but they didn't know any of that either.

"You are wrong about Annie," the sheriff said to her three brothers. "There is a reason for everything and you need to hear her reasons for not contacting you. Your sister is the most kindest, loving human being on this here earth. I know there is a hole in her heart for y'all, and y'all need to think about fixin' it."

Noble started sobbing. "I ain't no baby, sheriff. I cry a lot. It is a sickness, I know."

The sheriff walked over and put his arms around Noble. "Listen, son. I got a rent house in town that's empty. You and your brothers can come live in it until you get on your feet. Y'all are gonna need jobs, and the government is gonna be coming our way to repair our town and will be looking for people to hire. But for right now, let me get that medicine for you, okay? Do you have it written on a piece of paper somewhere?"

"Yessir, I do. Wait right cheer. I'll be right back."

Noble ran into the house to find the military prescription. Boone and Buddy walked over to the sheriff and patted him on the back. "Thank you, sir," Boone said, extending his hand for a shake.

"Thank you, Mr. Sheriff," Buddy said.

The sheriff nodded.

Then Buddy stuck out his right hand for a shake and he saw that the thumb and little finger were missing. The sheriff didn't hesitate and shook it.

Noble came running out of the house with the prescription. The sheriff told them he would be back tomorrow, weather permitting, and that he was going to talk to his wife about renting the house to them, and he was going to tell Annie about their situation.

They just hung their heads low and nodded.

All the way down the hill, the sheriff was on the brink of tears. The life that Annie's brothers have lived will surely upset her, he thought. But he knew she would want to help them.

And she did.

He stopped at her diner and told her all about them. She sobbed like someone had just died instead of being found. She wanted to go right up that torn-up hill and get them right then and there, but Sheriff Haynes told her she'd have to wait until tomorrow.

She could hardly sleep. Tomorrow couldn't come fast enough.

15
THE HEADLINES

Clyde was stacking boxes of Kellogg's Corn Flakes cereal on the top shelf of his store when Harlan and his wife, Cleo, brought the *Herndon Chronicle* for his racks.

"Got two more girls missin'," said Harlan, handing Clyde a paper.

Clyde stepped down from his short ladder and put the paper on the counter to read. Big, bold headlines said, "Highway snatcher back in action." An article and photographs of the latest victims took up half of the front-page. There was even a photo of the two sets of parents crying and hugging each other.

"They're just babies," said Clyde.

Harlan agreed. "I was jest sayin' that to Cleo. Don't remember this snatcher fella takin' such young ones b'fore. Both were 15. One girl had been gone a week before they reported it and the other had been gone two weeks."

"I suppose you've read this article, Harlan?" asked Clyde.

"Oh, yeah, Cleo read it out loud to me whilst I was drivin'."

"Did it say why the parents waited so long to call the police and report them missing?" Clyde asked. "Did they know each other?"

"No, they didn't know each other. The reporter interviewed both parents of each family and both girls had run away numerous times before, but always came back after a few days. When it got to be weeks instead of days, they filed a missing report. That's when several witnesses came forth and told the parents they saw each of the girls hitchhiking on the highway at different times."

"What highway is it?" asked Clyde.

"Both were hitching south on 51."

"Like, to Memphis? What were they thinking!" asked Clyde. "They are how old? Fifteen?"

"I know, Clyde," said Cleo. "The world is different than when we was young. Why, our daddys would've beat the tar out of our rears if we even hinted at runnin' away. And I don't ev'r remember wanting to, you know?"

"Yeah, I know," said Clyde. "There are a few teens that

come in here and are disrespectful."

"Well, we gotta go get us some grub over at the diner," said Harlan. "Then we gotta get on the road to Herndon. Say, have you got any of Annie's pecan muffins yet? Isn't it time for them? I always think of those damn muffins when the weather turns cool."

"Yeah, I've had a lot of people asking about them and her pies," Clyde said. "But, no, I don't have any. But you might ask her when you go over there. That tornado done threw our lives into a tailspin."

"That reminds me," said Cleo, "someone said y'all are getting government aid to fix up the town. That's really good news."

"Yes," said Clyde. "Wish it could bring back all the lives we lost, too. I think we are all in mourning around here, and these girls missing are just going to add to our fears and worries."

"Hope they find that sick bastard and cut off his you-know-what," said Cleo. "Wonder if it's the same guy from before? How long has it been? 1959? Can that be?"

"Yeah, 'bout '59, that we know of," said Harlan. "There's been a cold spell until now. That's nine years without a missing girl. We all thought the bastard had died."

"Well, he could have," said Clyde. "This could be a copycat."

The couple started to walk out of the store when Cleo turned around for one last thought about the missing girls. "You know, none of the missing girls' bodies have ever been found. Not even bone fragments. It's like this asshole eats them and puts their bones in a woodchipper."

"Awwwww, Cleo! Stop it!" said Harlan. "You've been reading too many of those *National Enquirers*. C'mon, let's go see Annie. She's always a bright light that cheers us up."

"That she is," said Clyde. "Say, ask her if she's got a leftover chicken pot pie. It's the best. And while you're there, place an order for a pecan pie or her muffins. She won't forget you, I guarantee."

16
BUDDY

Annie dropped the kids off at the front door of the school instead of letting them walk. She wanted to make sure they got safely inside before she drove over to the diner to meet Sheriff Haynes to drive up into the hills. Maybe they would use her truck or maybe the sheriff would drive, she wasn't sure. But she had a good 15 minutes to get the coffee perking, give Henry instructions about the day's menu, and put the biscuits in the oven before the sheriff arrived.

"I should be back by the time the kids get out of school, Henry," she said. "If not, they know to walk over here and wait for me. Is that okay with you?"

Henry smiled and gave her one of his famous winks. "You bet," he replied. "I'd do anything for you and them kids. Wouldn't have anything in my life if it waddn't for y'all."

Annie gave him a big hug. "I don't know what I'd do without you!" she said. Then she grabbed her thick sweater and an umbrella because it looked like it could be a downpour any minute.

"Hope that road ain't a washout for y'all," said a concerned Henry. "That would be hell bein' up in the hills with no way back down."

Annie sucked in a big breath and blew it out slowly. "Yeah, the sheriff will know what's best. Here he is now."

The bell on the diner's door rang when the sheriff entered. He took off his hat and smiled at Annie. "You ready, Mis' Annie?" he asked.

"Yes, Larry ... I mean sheriff."

He smiled at her respectful term.

"Do you think it's going to rain?" she asked. "Because I don't want to get stuck up in the hills if the rain washes out the road."

"I don't think that's gonna be a problem," he said. "Maybe into the night, but not this morning. We'll be back by noon. I heard on the news that the rain ain't comin' in until after five. We'll be down by then, ma'am."

She smiled at him and then shook her index finger in front of his nose. "Okay ... I'll be holding you to that, sir. Are we taking your vehicle or my truck?"

"My vehicle," he said. "Yore truck is too big and, pardon

me, ma'am, but I think my vehicle is more reliable."

They both laughed softly. She loved Larry Haynes. He was another one that she wished was her daddy.

They got in the car and Annie started cramping. She felt like she needed to go to the bathroom, but knew it was just nerves. "I'm just beside myself with nerves!" she admitted. "On one hand, I'm so very, very happy to see my brothers. But on the other hand, I don't know how to act. Should I act happy and all that when they have nothing? Or should I be sympathetic and crying? Because I can do both. I am feeling all of that and more."

The sheriff didn't say anything right away.

"What???" she asked. "What are you thinking I should do? Just blurt it out."

He looked over at her tears streaming down her cheeks and her hands shaking like she had done something wrong. "Annie, girl, I ain't ever seen you say or do something that waddn't right," he said. "Jest be yerself. Jest be you."

Annie put her head back on the seat and closed her eyes. She took in some deep breaths and then let them out slowly, just like she saw a woman do on some daytime television show. It helped calm herself down.

"Okay, Larry. I'm fine now," she said.

He reached over and grabbed her hand and squeezed it. "I knew you'd work it out. A gal like you and all you been through knows how to handle even the worst of things and come out a winner," he said.

She watched the sheriff maneuver the car on half a road, hugging the right side where Annie was sitting. She decided to close her eyes and then open them when he reached the whole road, and the sheriff agreed that it was the right thing for her to do.

"Now, Mis' Annie, I want you to know something," he said calmly.

Her eyes got so big that he thought they might pop out.

He laughed. "Naw, it ain't that scary, so calm yersef down," he said.

She covered her face with her hands and said, "What is it?"

The sheriff reached over and pulled her hands away from her face and said, "I just want you to know that even if this road got washed out, I know another way down."

Annie's mouth flew open. "What??? All this time you knew that and didn't tell me?" Then she hit his arm.

Sheriff Haynes laughed. "Listen, this here is a good thang. You being with your kin that you hadn't seen since you were what, twelve? This is exciting. But I want you know that they know nothing about you. They don't know about the Bartons and how you were a prisoner in their house. They think you just left and didn't want anything to do with them."

She smiled, "I know. I should have reached out to them sooner."

"No, that's not why I'm sayin' this to you," he said in a serious tone. "These young men have lived with your dad in a place not fit for pigs. There's only three of them here. I didn't ask where the other five were. And there's one more thing I didn't tell ya."

Annie looked at him and began her breathing treatments again. "And what is that, Larry? What could that possibly be?"

The sheriff looked straight ahead and said, "Yer daddy is dead."

Annie started laughing! "Oh, is that all? I already knew that! Dub told me that a long time ago. I guess he had to take the ambulance up there and take his body out of their house and down to the morgue in Herndon. But he never shared anything else with me, and I didn't ask."

The sheriff reached over and grabbed her hand. "Well, Mis' Annie, you had a full plate of worry goin' on in your own life. Don't be so sorry about that."

About a minute later, Sheriff Haynes stopped the car. "See over yonder where that sign is? The one that says Slayton?"

"Yeah," she replied. "But it's spelled wrong."

They both laughed, but it wasn't a funny laugh. It was a nervous, sad laugh.

"There, now. Feel better?" he asked.

"Yes. Let's go get them."

They walked across the road and entered the compound that was covered with overgrown trees and bushes. She could hardly see the house for all the clutter everywhere. But the closer she got, she could make out three blond men standing on the porch. Her throat started closing up and she could feel a good crying spell coming on. She stopped and reached for the sheriff's hand and he gripped it firmly. Tears ran down her face and her legs felt weak. She dropped to the ground and cried uncontrollably, and the young men ran to embrace her. They were crying, too, even wailing out loud for her.

She finally got ahold of her feelings enough to stand up and look each of them in the face. One by one, she touched their faces and wiped their tears with her hands. All of them were too emotional to even talk, but Annie found the strength to speak first.

"You look like Mama, Noble," she said, sniffing and blowing her nose on a handkerchief the sheriff gave her. "I saw you taking pictures one day across the creek."

"Yes, ma'am, that was me. How'd you know?" he asked.

She laughed with tears running into her mouth. "Your hair," she sobbed. "That tuft of hair that sticks up and won't lay down. It's called a cowlick. You were born with it. I knew it was you."

He hugged her and didn't want to let go. "I love you, Annie," he whispered in her ear.

All she could do was shake her head. It was just so emotional for everyone.

Then she looked at Boone. "I know this is you, Boone," she cried. "I saw you being born in Mama's bed."

"Huh?" he said. "I wuz jest a kid when you left."

"I know, sweet boy, but you have a birthmark below your ear. It's still there."

"Whut about me, Annie? Whut you know about me?" asked Edward.

Annie looked into Edward's eyes and said, "You, my sweet Edward, looked just like me when you were born. Mama even said, 'He could be yer twin, girl.' And I took care of you like I was your mama. You were my little shadow and Daddy was so jealous."

She reached for his hands and he pulled back. "What's going on, Edward? What's wrong with your hands?"

"Show her, Buddy, show her," urged Noble.

Edward lowered his head and held his hands out for Annie to see. Her mouth dropped and she cried out like she was in pain. She could hardly see through her tears, and took both of his hands and kissed them all over.

"Daddy did that to him," Noble said, angrily. "He wuz a basterd. He told Buddy how to set the trap wrong and it sprung back and got him. He was a basterd."

Sheriff Haynes finished his cigarette and joined them. Then they walked over to the picnic table to talk some more before leaving. They sat outside and talked about everything. Annie learned that her stepmother, Loretta, took the other five boys to Memphis and they hadn't heard from any of them since.

"Well, get your stuff together because you're going with me and the sheriff," she said. "He's got a house for y'all with running water. And we hear there will be jobs for you when the government starts building our town back."

It took no time for Annie's three brothers to gather up their belongings because they didn't really have anything worth taking. They climbed into the sheriff's car and stunk it up so badly they had to roll down the windows. But it wasn't raining, and Annie praised God for that.

Annie told Henry to put a "CLOSED" sign on the diner because her brothers were coming to her house for the night. She let them bathe in her bathroom and they put on clean shirts, overalls and underwear that Clyde brought from his store. Dwayne, Will and Becky were laughing with their uncles and asking so many questions. Annie was sure Becky was going to say something about Edward's hands that would offend him, but it turned out to be the sweetest thing of the night.

Edward reached for a piece of bread on the dinner table and when Becky saw that his fingers were missing, Annie's face scrunched up.

"Edward," said Becky.

He interrupted her and said, "Call me Buddy."

"Okay," she replied. "Buddy, how'd your hands get like

that?"

He pulled them into his lap and put his head down.

"Don't be sad, Buddy," she said. "Let me see them."

Buddy didn't move.

"C'mon," she insisted, "let me see them."

Buddy pulled one hand up and set it down on the table next to her. "My daddy made them get cut."

Becky made an outline of his hand with her finger. "Hmmmm … you know what, Buddy?"

"Whut?" he said quietly.

"It don't matter that you don't have a thumb or a baby finger. The fingers you got now are the best ones to have."

"Why you say that?" he asked.

"Because thumbs don't do nothing. Baby fingers don't do nothing. But the fingers you have in the middle can do a lot."

Everyone at the table started clapping and smiling and shouting good things. "Yea, Buddy! Yea, Buddy" they said over and over.

Becky stood up and leaned over to give Buddy a hug.

And Buddy hugged back.

"You are a special person," she whispered in his ear.

"Because you are my uncle and I love you just the way you are."

17
THE MESSAGE

Annie walked toward the creek with her hot tea in her hand. It was still dark, but she loved this time of morning. It was cool, almost cold, but she was wearing pajamas, socks, slippers and a chenille robe. Around her neck was a scarf that she grabbed off the back porch before descending the stairs to the back yard.

The barren land leading to the creek was lined with small clumps of soil that had been turned up by a backhoe. Government workers had been removing the debris along the bank and in the fields and depositing it into trucks that carried the waste to the garbage dump outside Cook's city limits. Many of her customers at Pig Dog Diner shared stories about the junk that was dredged up onto the banks, things that didn't look like they belonged on Earth. They talked about invaders from Mars or some other planet and how the Martians were responsible for the tornado and the weird, twisted metal found along Pig Dog.

A recent rain created a flow of water in the creek and Annie's thoughts turned to the joy her sacred place provided. She smiled when she thought how the area could possibly return to normal now, but it was going to take some time. The trees and bushes lining the creek would take years to grow back, and there was an emptiness that tugged at her heart. The animals were gone – no turtles, birds, squirrels, raccoons. No kudzu or leaves on any of the branches. The tornado had blown them all into the next county. She thought about Lem Smithers' words when he saw the damage.

"Damndest thang I e'vr sar," Lem said while surveying the land. "I ain't heered tell of no tornado ev'r jumping into ah hole like a crick and ridin' it. Them 'nados jump *ov'r* holes. Not jump in."

Annie knew firsthand that the creek was not like any other creek in the county or the state or the world, for that matter. There were forces within it that changed peoples' lives, and she had been one of them. How could she tell her family, friends and customers that she is positive it's not Martians? That it's a spirit of nature or essence of a person?

"No, they'd never buy that!" she said, laughing.

While sitting on a tree stump and drinking her hot tea, she wondered what the creek would tell her next.

"What journey are you going to take me on this time?" she said aloud softly, watching the small amount of water trickle over the rocks and provide a hypnotic sound. The peaceful feeling made her so relaxed that she thought she might just lie down and take a catnap. But she fought the sensation and stayed awake. Her eyes scanned the other side of the creek and she could see glowing eyes of critters that made her smile.

"Come back little critters," she said sweetly.

The moon above began to make way for the sun's turn at the day, and she could see movement across the creek. She sat still to keep from being noticed as the animals came out from behind the tree trunks one by one and headed toward the water.

Annie looked at the deep crevice and wondered how they were going to get down into the creek's hole that the tornado had dug even deeper. But they did! It was such a beautiful sight seeing the squirrels running around and around the trees, the turtles trudging forward across the unsettled bank, and the possums and raccoons cautiously finding their way down to the creek's level below them.

Waterbirds flew down from out of nowhere, frogs hopped off the bank into the water, and snakes slithered down the bank's slope. Annie was overcome with joy. She continued to wait for the creek to give her a sign. When it looked like nothing was going to happen, she got up to leave. When she did, a light wind started to blow. It began at her feet and worked its way around her body like a mini tornado. It had been years since she felt the wind that she first thought was going to turn her to salt. This time she knew better, and quickly closed her eyes while it whipped around her. After it calmed down and dissipated, she opened her eyes to see if anything had been left in its path. But there was nothing.

The sun came out in full force and cast a glow on something near her. She walked over to it, hoping to find a significant treasure like she did when she found the book six years earlier, but it was just a tin can. She picked it up hoping to find something inside, but there was nothing.

The tin can, however, jarred her memory! It reminded her of the container she found after the tornado hit. She'd forgotten all about the tin box with the padlock on it! Goosebumps began at her thighs and moved up to her neck. She took off running toward the house. When she reached the back steps, she was out of breath.

"Dang!" she said screamed. "Where'd I put that damn thing?"

Dwayne opened the back door and startled her.

"Where you been, Mama?" he asked. "Can we have breakfast now?"

With her heart about to pound itself out of her chest, she answered slowly, "Yes … hon. You … want cereal … or eggs today?"

18
MARTY

A cold snap right before Halloween changed everyone's mood from being active outside and energetic to hunkering down inside near their fireplaces and stoves. Temporary housing for displaced citizens affected by the tornado was complete, and rebuilding Cook's east side of town was taking on a new personality. The Baptist Church's building doubled in size and its steeple was now one of the largest in the state. Storm cellars were put in every new structure, and many of the homes that weren't destroyed got a fair deal for adding a storm cellar to their property.

Annie took advantage of that deal and inquired about one for her diner. She thought it would not only benefit her family, but many of Cook's citizens who could not afford a shelter on their existing property. A company called Anderson & Sons Storm Cellars came out to look over the diner's property to determine if there was enough land for the size bunker she wanted. Because the remodeled kitchen now expanded into that yard space, the only area they could dig was behind the garage.

Annie signed an agreement that it was okay for them to proceed. The bank approved her small business loan and work began shortly thereafter.

One day after the lunch crowd left, Annie was making pecan muffins and pies in the diner's kitchen when one of the workers came in. She heard the door's bell ring and looked up from stirring her muffin batter to see the handsome man, whose arm muscles were the largest she had ever seen. Their eyes met, and she put down her spoon and went into the dining room to see what he needed.

"Hello, ma'am," the young man said, extending his hand for a shake. "My name is Marty. My uncle is Clyde Tubbs. He wanted me to come in to introduce myself to you."

Annie's hand was swallowed up by Marty's, but he was gentle when he shook it. "It's very nice to meet you, Marty," she said. "I was wondering when we were going to meet."

Marty smiled. "So my uncle told you about me?"

She blushed. "Yes! He said you could fix anything!"

This time it was his turn to blush. "Well, I don't know about that. I am having some difficulty out back with your bunker. Looks like we've got to dig a little closer to the diner's foundation than what we originally said, and I just need permission to do that."

Annie didn't even give it a second thought. If Marty says it needs to be dug closer, then that's what will have to be done.

Simple as that. "Of course, Marty. I trust that you know what you're doing."

"Thank you, Mis' Annie," he said. "We should have the digging done by tomorrow and it won't interrupt your business. If the bunker was going to be built on the diner's side of your building and not the garage side, there would be a problem. But that's not the case, so we're okay."

Annie was impressed with his politeness. "Do what you have to do, Marty. And when you're done, come in and have dinner. Are you working alone?"

"No, ma'am, I have two other workers with me," he replied.

"No problem," she said. "I will be happy to feed them, free of charge, of course.

"That's awfully nice of you, Mis' Annie," he said. "We'll see you later!"

He started to walk out the door when she shouted, "Do you prefer roast beef or fried chicken? Because I can change the menu for tonight if you've got a preference."

Marty was even more wowed by her. "Whatever you've got planned is fine, ma'am. We are not particular. We are all bachelors, so we are used to eating hamburgers and hot dogs!"

"I can cook that, too!" Annie said, laughingly.

"You are just the nicest lady," he said sweetly. "It has been a real pleasure meeting you. See you later!"

He opened the door to leave, but then stopped and held it open for someone approaching. It was Dub. Annie hadn't seen him in weeks. She was a little nervous when he walked in. She smelled whiskey as soon as he came through the door.

"Hey, Dub," she said softly. "Where have you been? Are you doing okay?"

"No, Annie, I'm not," he said sternly. "Who just left here? Another man that wants to get in your pants?"

"Dub! What's got into you? That's a horrible thing to say to me."

"I'm sorry, I guess," he said sarcastically. "I'm just tired."

Annie's hands were trembling. "Why? What's going on?"

"Just work," he replied. "Lots of work. If I'm not running the ambulance, I'm pulling cars with the wrecker. I'm behind in my farm chores. It's just too much lately."

Annie tried to feel sorry for him, but she just couldn't get passed the remark about 'another man that wants to get in your pants.'

"Have you thought about hiring someone to help you?" she asked, but really didn't care if he answered.

"Naw," he replied. "I don't trust these young people to do my business."

"Can I get you something to eat?" she asked.

"Yeah, just a sandwich. I gotta take it with me, so wrap it in waxed paper."

"Coming right up," she said while walking back to the kitchen prep area.

Annie opened the refrigerator to find the leftover tuna salad from lunch. She bent over to move some items on the bottom shelf when she felt him behind her and then his hands on her breasts. She let out a yell and stood up. He groped her from behind, this time between the legs.

She wrestled free and turned toward him, pushing him off and reaching for a knife on the counter. "So help me, God," she screamed, wielding the knife in the air, "if you touch me again, you'll have this knife in your craw."

He put his hands up in the air and backed off. The bell on the door rang and he turned around and slowly walked out the door. Marty entered and saw her holding the knife. She put it down and sobbed.

"That was Dub, wasn't it?" he asked.

Annie nodded.

"What can I do, Mis' Annie? Do you want me to call the sheriff?" he asked.

"No," she replied. "I don't want to agitate him more. What can I do for you, Marty? Are you wanting to eat now? Because I can whip up anything for you and your crew."

"That's awfully nice of you, but we are calling it a day," he said. "We just uncovered some human bones in the yard and are waiting for the authorities to arrive. They need to come right away while the dig is fresh and before an animal runs off with them or bad weather sets in."

Annie started to cry uncontrollably. She reached into her apron's pocket and pulled out a handkerchief to blow her nose. "Can't *anything* be simple or normal in this stupid town? All I wanted was a bunker and I had to choose the spot where someone was probably murdered? *Really?* What is it with this town and skeleton bones?"

He stepped toward her and she fell into his arms for comfort. It was awkward being in the arms of a stranger, but she needed some consoling.

Marty patted her back and started telling her what to expect. "There, there, Mis' Annie. Please try to take a deep breath and muster up some strength for these guys that are coming out. This is not my first bones discovery, so I know the authorities are going to want to know who built this place, who has owned it over time, and if you know of someone who has gone missing over the years."

Annie told Marty that her late husband's father, Minner Brown, built Tinker's Tow & Garage in the late 1930s. Then Minner's Uncle James bought it and ran it until his health went bad and he died, leaving Tinker's Tow to Annie and her husband,

Robert, who was in a coma and died before he even knew it was his.

"Well, that's all good to know," said Marty. "Did any of them hire workers to run the place in their absence? Like, for instance, who drives those vehicles parked in the garage?"

"Oh, those belong to Dub. He owns them and uses the garage to park them in," she explained.

"How long has he been doing that?" Marty asked.

Annie thought for a moment. "I don't know the answer to that question, but Dub wouldn't hurt a flea."

"Mis' Annie," he said calmly, "are we talking about the same man that just came in here drunk, and the same man that you were about to stab with a butcher knife?"

Annie thought for a moment before she answered. She began to weep again while trying to justify Dub's actions. "You know, Marty, that man loves me and I do not love him in the same way. He would never hurt me or my kids and I blame myself for his excessive alcohol use. He is frustrated and depressed, and I don't know what to do because I am in love with someone else."

Marty let out a big sigh. "Okay, listen. Don't hold back with these guys that are coming to talk to you. They are good at what they do. They will weed out who is suspicious and who isn't. They will talk to other people in town and do a thorough job. So don't worry about this, okay? You are not the guilty person here. You inherited this through family. Those bones were not in a fresh grave. They appear to have been there many years."

Annie looked at the clock on the wall and told Marty her kids would be there any minute from school. "Please don't mention this to them," she said. "I will take them over to Clyde's store and get them some ice cream, and my sitter, Lindy Sue, can walk them home and stay with them until I get there."

"That's a good idea," Mis' Annie. And you will want to close the diner for the night."

"How long do you think the investigation will take?" she asked.

"I don't rightly know," he replied. "They will rope off the area and dig up the bones first, then take them to a lab. But I'm pretty sure it won't just stop there. They'll probably dig up the whole yard back there and under the foundation. But once they get the bones dug up and out of here, you will be able to open your business. Field agents will arrive to talk to people in the community to try and figure out who the bones might belong to. I'm thinking you'll be back in business in about two or three days."

Annie saw her children walking through the door and wiped her eyes with her apron.

"Hey, Mama!" Dwayne yelled as he came through the door. Will and Becky followed behind him carrying their books and placing them on one of the tables.

Annie came out from around the counter to greet them. Marty watched her kiss their faces and stroke their hair. They weren't like most kids, who slapped their mother's hand away and wiped the kisses from their faces with the back of their hands. Annie's children were genuinely happy to see her and returned the affection.

She kneeled down and looked up in their faces. "I need y'all to go over to Clyde's and get an ice cream or soda and wait for Lindy Sue to come get you and take you home," she said.

"But why, mama? We can help you get ready for dinner," said Will.

"That's so sweet of you, darlin', but Mama's not cooking dinner tonight. I am going to close the diner for the evening. The men digging our tornado bunker came across a problem in the yard and it needs to be fixed first before they can continue."

She handed Dwayne a dollar for ice cream. "And if you're really good, like I know you always are, you can stay up and watch *Daniel Boone* tonight on the TV.

"*Bewitched, too?*" asked Dwayne.

"We'll see," said Annie. "Now, shoo! I will see you later, okay?"

"Okay, Mama," they said in unison while running out the door.

Fifteen minutes later, Lindy Sue's bus from Herndon High School dropped her off at the schoolyard. She walked over to the diner like she did every day to see if Annie needed her to babysit. Marty was still there drinking a cup of coffee and waiting for the authorities who had to drive up from Memphis, which was about 90 minutes from Cook.

Annie started to introduce Lindy Sue to Marty when the teenager interrupted her.

"Oh, we already know each other," said Lindy Sue. "His daddy and my daddy are friends. But I haven't seen you in a really long time, Marty! Where have you been?"

Marty stood up and hugged Lindy Sue. "I went off to college," he said. "I got a job designing and installing tornado bunkers after graduation, and here I am back in tornado alley," he laughed.

"I think you mean tornado creek," laughed Annie.

"Yeah, you're right," said Marty. "That was a real freak of nature for sure."

Lindy Sue left to get the kids at Clyde's store and walk them home. Annie put on another pot of coffee for the forensic authorities that were driving up from Memphis. They arrived at four-thirty and immediately began excavating the land. It was dark by six o'clock, so they covered the dirt with large canvases and roped it off. Then they drove to Herndon to spend the night.

Marty peeked his head in the door and said, "We'll be back tomorrow, Mis' Annie."

"Wait!" she hollered. "I've got some roast beef sandwiches for you and your guys. You can eat 'em in the car. You've just got to be hungry!"

He *was* hungry and so were his workers. "You didn't have to do that," he said, "but we're mighty happy for your hospitality."

He took the brown bag and began walking toward the door. Then he stopped and turned around to face her. "I'll be back in the morning to see what kind of progress is being made," he said. "Goodnight, ma'am."

"Goodnight, Marty. See you tomorrow."

19
FAMILY

Tongues were waggin' all over Cook the next morning about the bones found behind the diner. It was on the front-page of the *Herndon Chronicle* newspapers, and the store sold out in one hour. Clyde had to tell Harlan and Cleo to increase his delivery count until the whole bones thing was solved.

The story stirred up memories of Maydell Stokes' skeleton hanging on a tree root in Pig Dog Creek, and Cook, Tennessee, was listed as a "haunting place to live" in the Herndon paper and on the nightly news. Reporters also cited the strange "phenomenon" of a tornado that rode out part of the creek, and quoted meteorologists who could not explain the unnatural occurrence.

Anchors and reporters on the national TV news made fun of the creek's name, showing interviews with people who referred to the residents as hillbillies and unsophisticated yokels. The names infuriated Clyde. When a reporter came into the store to interview him, he lashed out at him and was captured in a state of rage by the photographer, who ran the photo on the next day's front-page.

The day after that, it was Buddy's picture. An undercover photographer took a photo of Buddy stacking the shelves in Clyde's store with his "claw hands." The caption read, "Is there something in Pig Dog Creek's water that's mutating Cook's residents?"

Clyde was hopping mad. "Everything is going to hell in a hand basket," he yelled, after seeing Buddy's picture on the front page.

And then it snowed six inches and things quieted down. By the time the roads were passable, Cook's otherworldly oddities were old news.

Annie was ready to say good riddance to the stories about the bones on her property, but she was not going to let the newspaper get away with the unkind photo and caption about Buddy's hands. She wrote a scathing letter to the *Herndon Chronicle*, which did not publish it. So she sent it to the mayor.

A week later she received a certificate from the mayor with Buddy's name on it. *"This certificate certifies that Edward "Buddy" Slayton is the recipient of the Good Neighbor Award for his service and perseverance to the community of Cook during a time of discord and inaccuracy."*

It wasn't exactly an apology, but "inaccuracy" was good

enough for Annie. Clyde framed the award and put it behind the counter. Buddy was an instant celebrity in Cook.

After being closed for almost a week, Annie's diner was given the go-ahead to open. The "collectors," as the residents called them, believed that they had extracted all the bones from the diner's property. They never formally announced if they had found more than the original bones that Marty unearthed, and the investigators were still trying to reach many of the residents who lived up in the hills to inquire about any missing friends or relatives within the past 20 years.

Annie was given the OK to open the diner, and that meant Henry could get back to work and so could she. It was great being home with the kids, but she missed the interaction with Cook's residents, and she hadn't been able to see Jonathan Shea during that time because of the weather and the kids being at home. But, thank goodness for telephone calls! She was able to stay in touch with him daily while she waited to go back to work.

Dub hadn't been around either since the day he came into the diner when Marty was walking out. Annie was worried about his disposition, and told herself she was going to visit his farm over the weekend. She imagined that his wrecker service was overwhelmed with calls to pull people out of ditches during the snowstorm, because the truck was not parked in the diner's garage. She missed him, and was sorry for what happened the day that she was going to strike him with a knife.

She missed the old Dub who was always checking on her and the kids. Not a day went by without talking to him. But something changed, and Annie wasn't sure if it was his fault or hers.

"Where is Mr. Dub, Mama?" Will asked her one day.

Annie searched her mind for a good answer before replying. "Well, I don't rightly know for sure, but I think Mr. Dub has a lot of chores on his farm to do and a lot of animals to feed and lots of people to tend to with the ambulance and wrecker service. He's just been really busy helping others right now."

Will seemed satisfied with that answer. "Yeah, I know he is busy, Mama, but he needs to take time to come see us. We are his family, too."

"You're right, pumpkin," she said, pinching Will's sweet little cheeks. "Maybe we'll ride out to his farm soon and check on him."

"Yeah, Mama! Dub needs a checkup!"

They both laughed.

Annie suspected that Dub finally realized that her heart belonged to another. The night that she and Jonathan Shea made love in her bedroom was the night that any dreams of a future with Dub ended, and he knew it. That night's passion caused Dub to stake out her home and hurl questions and accusations the next day about Jonathan's Jeep, and it was probably the reason he had whiskey on his breath in the middle of the day and why he was groping her in the diner.

With Thanksgiving a few weeks away and Christmas

holidays after that, Annie decided to step up her "giving" ways and host an event sponsored by the diner. Over the past year, Cook's residents had suffered with the tornado, rebuilt their community, discovered human bones on the diner's property, and experienced bad press locally and nationally. She gathered the kids around the kitchen table to brainstorm.

"What can we do, kids? Who can we help?" she asked them.

"The soldiers, Mama," said Dwayne. "I see them all the time on TV."

"Okay," said Annie, writing the suggestion down on a writing tablet.

"The poor people, Mama," said Will. "There are kids in my school with no shoes."

"Good idea, son," said Annie. She turned to look at Becky who was wearing a very sad face. "Becky? Do you have an idea in that pretty little head?"

Becky wasn't too sure if she should bring it up. She spoke quietly, almost whispering. "Free haircuts, Mama. One of my friends has bugs in his hair and a lot of my friends get their mama to cut their hair."

"Good idea, hon," said Annie.

"What about you, Mama? What do you want to do?" asked Dwayne.

"They are all good ideas!" Annie said. "But we just need one. What is it that all of these people cannot live without?"

They thought for a minute and then Will said, "Food, Mama. Food."

"You're right, hon!" said Annie. "Let's think about feeding people. Maybe we order some frozen turkeys and give them away. Or maybe we just have one day of non-stop feeding people free at the diner."

"We need a bigger place," said Will.

"Okay, how about your school's dining room?" she asked.

"Yeah!" said Dwayne. "It's a huge room with tables and chairs. That will work, Mama! That will work!"

Becky started pouting. "That's not any fun, Mama. Can we add some fun?"

"Sure, baby girl. What kind of fun are you thinking about?"

A big smile broke out on Becky's face. "A carnival, like on that TV commercial. Games, and prizes, and balloons and candy."

They all got excited! The boys started beating on the table with their fists, and saying, "Yes, Mama, Yes! Yes, Mama, Yes! "Yes, Mama, Yes!"

So, their Mama said yes!

20
UNCLE TITUS

A few days passed with slushy snow, then watery roads and dripping roofs, and then, finally, the remnants of the frozen precipitation was gone – like six inches just never happened. Thanksgiving was just around the corner and that meant Christmas was not too far away. Annie's kids were getting excited about cutting down a tree to decorate.

The diner was a hub of activity. Residents were placing orders for Annie's pecan muffins and pies, and others were dropping off donations to the annual Christmas party at the school that Annie volunteered to help sponsor and chair. Henry and Lindy Sue were working long hours, and Marty and his crew were just about finished with the tornado shelter.

Noble and Boone got jobs working on a new bridge over the Mississippi River that was scheduled to begin in February.

When finished, the bridge would carry Interstate drivers across the river and connect Missouri and Tennessee directly. The brothers were excited about being a part of something so grand, and were already enrolled in training classes.

But the best news of all was Buddy's new hands. After seeing his photograph on the front-page of the *Herndon Chronicle*, two doctors in Memphis put their heads together and created gloves for Buddy to wear that included thumbs and little fingers built inside that fit tightly over the stubs of his damaged digits.

No one smiles more than Buddy in the entire state of Tennessee.

And in the midst of all the celebratory preparation that the approaching holidays were bestowing on her, Annie received a telephone call that her Uncle Titus had died and the funeral was being held in two days.

"I don't even know this man," she said to Henry. "He's my mama's oldest brother but he had a different mother. I guess maybe I knew him when I was a little girl, but he always seemed so old. He isn't anyone to me now, you know?"

Henry had a smirk on his face. "He's family, Mis' Annie," he said. "Your kids need to go and meet other family members. It will be good for you and them. You'll see."

Annie shrugged her shoulders. "I guess," she sighed. "Can you take care of things while I'm gone? It will just be one day. We'll leave early and get back late. It's in a little town just north of Memphis."

"No problem, Mis' Annie. No problem," said Henry.

She gave Jonathan Shea a call to let him know where she was going. They talk daily over the phone, sometimes twice, and each morning he stops for "coffee and kisses," as he calls it. He eats supper there on Tuesdays and Thursdays because he doesn't work late on those days, but a second overnight stay at her house has not happened yet. They almost got caught doing the hanky-panky when Henry arrived early for his morning shift at the diner and found them in the bathroom off the diner's kitchen.

Annie's children were happy to go on a road trip, even if it meant seeing relatives they didn't know they had. The weather was cold, but not frigid. Sunny, but not hot. It was actually a perfect day to travel.

The funeral was scheduled for 11:30 in the morning, and they pulled up to the church at 11 o'clock. She didn't see any faces that she recognized, but she was excited about meeting everyone in person at Uncle Titus' sister's house after the burial.

Will was extremely uncomfortable at the funeral. Annie wasn't sure if he had heard some horrible things at school about death or seen something on the television that disturbed him. He openly cried during the service and Annie had to walk him outside. He was an emotional child and maybe she should have prepared him better, she thought. He begged not to go to the cemetery, so they waited at the gate for everyone to leave so they could follow the cars to her Aunt Myrtle's house for the reception. Myrtle was Uncle Titus's sister, and a half-sister to Annie's mother, who was much younger. Annie began to get fidgety about meeting these estranged family members for the first time.

Myrtle's house was beautiful. She married into a nice family and had four daughters with her husband, Walter. However, Annie was unaware that one of their girls had been missing for 15 years and was presumed dead. Annie picked up a photo of Myrtle's family from atop the television set in the living room and said how much Lurleen looked like her own mother. That's when Myrtle told her how long she'd been missing.

"That was my heartbreak," said Myrtle, pointing to her daughter's image in the photo. "It has aged me and sickened my heart. Keep your children safe, Annie. Always know where they are and who they are with. Lurleen was just 14. She trusted everyone. Even the stranger who picked her up when she was hitchhiking."

Will looked up at Annie with tears flowing down his cheeks. She bent down to hear his whispered voice.

"Is she dead, Mama?" he said softly.

Annie knelt down to his level and nodded.

Will hugged her neck and Annie felt the wetness of his tears on her skin. She stood up and looked down into his eyes. "Wipe your eyes, sweetie," she said, handing him her handkerchief. "She is with our Lord, remember? He is taking care of her now. There isn't any better care than that anywhere on earth."

Annie took Will's hand and led him down a hall where she knew a bathroom would be. "Let's go put some cool water on your face, hon," she said.

On their way, they passed a room that Annie just knew was Lurleen's. She stopped and stared at all the frilly bedding and decorative windows. The whole room was like a shrine to Lurleen. Photos on the wall showed her at every age, and teddy bears of every size and color decorated the furniture, floor and shelves.

"Those were from the memorial," said Myrtle, who was standing behind them.

"Oh, Myrtle! You startled me. I hope you don't think that we …"

Myrtle cut her short. "No, hon, I want everyone to see this room. You are welcome to come in here. This room helped me with my grieving. I would walk by it and pretend that she was at school or on her way home. Sometimes, I would lay on the bed and put the pillows up against my back and pretend she was laying next to me. This room has helped me heal, if that's such a thing, because I don't think I'll ever heal completely."

This time it was Annie who was getting choked up. Will seemed to be just fine with all of Lurleen's things. It was like she was alive and it made him not so sad. Annie's favorite was the large portrait over the bed. "She is so beautiful!" said Annie.

"She favors my mama," said Myrtle.

"I am so embarrassed, Myrtle. I don't know who your mama was. All I know is that you and Uncle Titus are related to my mother, that y'all had the same daddy but not the same mama. I left my family when I was twelve."

Myrtle looked startled. "Twelve? Where'd you go?"

Annie's face turned red. "It's a long story, Aunt Myrtle."

Will tugged at Annie's skirt and said he had to go to the bathroom. "Now, Mama!"

Annie started to walk out with him, but he said he could go by himself. She turned around toward Myrtle and apologized. "I am so sorry, Myrtle. This is your brother's funeral and reception and we aren't talking about that loss. I apologize."

Myrtle started laughing one of those hysterical laughs that brings tears to your eyes and you can't stop. "Girl, my brother was the biggest bigot," she said. "He had meanness in his bones and caused us all kinds of pain. Then he got cancer and we couldn't wait for him to meet his maker."

Annie knew that feeling. She thought she was the only one that felt that way about anyone. "I understand," she said.

While they waited for Will to return, Annie's eyes, again, focused on the portrait. "That's a beautiful necklace she's wearing. Is it a family heirloom?"

Myrtle walked over to the painting and outlined the necklace with her fingers. "That was also my mama's," she said. "Lurleen had it on the day she disappeared. She had been drinking at a birthday party and got in a fight with her boyfriend. She wouldn't get in the car with him and started walking on the road. He begged and begged for her to get in the car, so he says. But I think he just threw up his hands and said, 'Just walk then.' And then took off. When she went missing, someone came forward and said they had seen her up on the highway hitchhiking. No tellin' what the sick bastard did to her when he picked her up."

"You know for sure that it was a man?" Annie asked.

"Naw," said Myrtle. "But who else could it have been? It was either a man or an animal attacked her. Because she is dead. I know she is dead. I don't feel her heart beating inside me anymore. I know you think that's probably crazy, but I felt her heartbeat when she was in my belly, and I kept feeling it until she died."

Walter peeked his head in the door. He was holding Will's hand. "Would each of you ladies like a date to take you to the dessert table? Because I hear you have to be on the arm of a man to partake of the fixins."

Myrtle and Annie started laughing. Then Myrtle put on a fake drawl. "Why, Mr. Smith, I'd be honored," she said, hooking her arm through his and walking out of the room.

Annie looked down at Will and he had his arm stuck out for her to hold.

"Why, Mr. Barton, I'd be happy to be your date," she said.

Will blushed. "Aww, Mama," he said. "I love you more than anything in this world. Anything, Mama. Anything!"

Annie bent down and cupped his cheeks with her hands. "I love you, more," she said.

He started to shake his head in disagreement and she held

it still with her hands. "Mamas always love their kids more, and this is why: You came from my belly. My body held you until you were perfectly formed and ready for this world. There is no gift greater than creating a child."

"Is that why Mrs. Myrtle has this room?"

"Yes, baby, because loving your babies doesn't ever stop, even when you know they aren't ever coming home."

21
THE GIFT OF GIVING

Cook, Tennessee, never looked more beautiful than it did in December 1968. Most of the town had been rebuilt after the tornado and new features were added to the terrain as a result. New streetlights, storefronts and homes displayed the holiday season's festive colors and looked like a scene from a cover of *Woman's Day Magazine.*

Lights, evergreen boughs with red velvet ribbons, handmade wreaths on doors and manger scenes dotted the community, providing happiness with their celebration of Jesus and Christianity. Annie hired a sign painter who wrote "Merry Christmas" on one of Pig Dog Diner's picture windows, and he created a snowman on the other window.

But the most beautiful feeling of the season was in the hearts of the residents. At the annual Christmas party that Annie organized at the school, many of Cook's poverty-stricken residents were showered with food, gifts, services and clothing. Annie's children said they didn't want anything for Christmas except to give to those in need, and their classmates received shoes, clothing, food and haircuts!

Everything was running smoothly, but the two missing girls from Herndon hadn't been found yet. There was no telling where those girls were, and all anyone could do was pray for the law enforcement to find them, and for the Lord to protect them until they could be found and brought home.

Annie didn't know the missing girls, but every time someone brought them up in a conversation, all she could see in her mind was Lurleen's face in the portrait hanging in her bedroom's shrine.

The December sky had been dreary all month, with low rainfall and no snow. Gray clouds kept the temperature down, averaging about 49-55 degrees during the day and dropping to the mid-thirties overnight. The weathermen were calculating a cold January and February for most of the northwestern portion of Tennessee, so everyone in Cook was enjoying the precipitation-free month while it lasted.

Annie's business was doing well. Her diner and properties were profitable and she was thinking about hiring another person to help Henry so she could spend more time at home with the kids and with Jonathan Shea.

The Memphis couple that had been renting her house next door for two years gave her a 30-day notice saying they would be moving out by Dec. 31. She immediately posted the information on Clyde's bulletin board in his store because she knew that most everyone checks the board for one thing or another. And, sure enough, Marty saw it and asked if he could rent it. He said he'd like to move in around the second week of January, if that was okay with Annie. She thought that it was a perfect bachelor pad, considering the house had just one bedroom and a one-stall carport. She always wondered how Verneice and her mother lived comfortably in that small house all those years.

With Christmas just a little over a week away, Annie decided to drive out to Dub's farm and take him a pie and some of Henry's fried chicken. The kids were still in school for a few more days, but she wanted to go without them to see what frame of mind Dub was in and why it had been eight weeks since she had seen him. He wasn't parking his emergency vehicles in her diner's garage anymore, and that baffled her. But she knew he was still alive because Pastor Russell saw him at a reclaim center in Herndon where residents who suffered property loss during the tornado could sort through all the items that were cleaned, tagged and ready to be claimed by their rightful owners. The pastor was curious about Dub's presence there.

"His homestead wasn't affected by that tornado, was it Mis' Annie?" he asked after church one Sunday.

Annie was speechless. Did the pastor think Dub was stealing items for himself or to sell for profit? "No, sir, his property wasn't hit at all by the tornado. Just strong winds that broke a few windows and loosened some boards on his barn."

The preacher looked at her with a puzzled face. She reacted quickly.

"Oh, you know Mr. Dub," she said, lightly slapping the pastor on the upper arm. "He's always doing things for other people. I bet he was looking for some things to return to folks who weren't able to drive to Herndon."

The preacher smiled and agreed. "Yes, you're right, Mis' Annie. What would we do in this community without the generosity and kindness of our citizens who help others? Like yourself! I am so pleased with your service to the Lord and all the people of Cook that you helped at the holiday event at the school."

Annie's face blushed. "It was my pleasure, Pastor Russell."

All the way to Dub's farm, she contemplated asking him why he was in Herndon at the reclaim center. She practiced over and over what she was going to say and then decided at the last minute to just let it go. She drove down the narrow road to his property and saw the barn door open and both of his emergency vehicles inside. The property looked to be somewhat neglected, like he had been gone for a few months. His prize cow was in a pen outside the barn, and the smell of animal feces made it hard to breathe. She rolled up the window, put her hankie to her nose and laid on the horn.

Dub came running out of the house. She hardly recognized him. He had long hair, a beard, and a pencil-thin body.

He was holding his pants up because they were too large for his thin frame. If she had met him on the streets of Herndon, she would have thought he was a panhandler and given him a few coins. As he approached her, she rolled down her window and rested her arm on the door. He smelled as bad as the cow.

"Whut are you doin' out heer?" he asked sternly.

She could tell he was mad because the veins in his neck were protruding.

"Is that any way to welcome a friend of yours to your property? What am I doing out here? Well, I am checking on you to see if you are still alive, that's what."

"Well, now you know I am, so jest tern yer truck 'round and go back the way you come," he said.

He started walking back inside and she turned the truck off and jumped out. "I am not leaving until you and I are back on solid ground!" she shouted. "Do you hear me, Dub Thomas? We are going to talk about our relationship right now! I miss you, the kids miss you. What's going on?"

He turned around to face her and put his hands on his hips. Then he lifted his right hand to run his fingers like a comb through his long greasy hair. "What the hell do you think is going on? Are you that stupid? Oh, wait. Yeah, you are. You never went to school, but you act all high and mighty, and then you spread yer legs for that doctor fella, forgettin' all 'bout how I took care of y'all when you was livin' with Robert and his piece of shit parents who were fucking you over. How I helped you get out of that shit hole.

I'm done with you, Miss High & Mighty. My life is about over, too."

He turned his back on her and started walking toward the front door. She started crying. He stopped walking and just stood facing the door while she cried.

"What do you mean your life is about over?" she said loudly with a choked-up throat.

He just stood there with his back to her.

"What do you mean?" she asked again, inching toward him.

He turned to face her. Tears were dripping down his face. "I'm losing the farm," he said. "I ain't worked in two months. Some smart aleck kid in Menlow took all my business. I couldn't pay you for the garage rent and I had no money for gas for the vehicles."

Annie started crying harder. He didn't budge. She took out a hankie and blew her nose. She watched him wipe his eyes with his grimy hands. She knew she had to save him from self-destructing. "Can we please talk this out?" asked Annie. "Because I think I can help you get all of it back."

Dub fell to his knees sobbing. "You don't owe me, Annie."

"Yes, I do. I owe you my life, Dub. So please, let's talk about this. I will wait in the truck for you while you shower. Then you are following me home in the wrecker and we're putting it up in the garage. Tomorrow we'll come back for the ambulance. After dinner and after the kids have settled down, we are going to plot out a plan on my kitchen table about how you can get your life back in order."

A smile broke out on his face. He turned around and went into the house. Twenty minutes later, he fired up the wrecker and followed her home.

22
THE DEAL

Annie's house was busting at the seams with relatives and friends on Christmas Day. In addition to her three children and three brothers, there was Henry and the new cook, Jeb, Jonathan Shea, Dub, and her brother Boone's new girlfriend, Carla Jean.

She and Henry had cooked everything the day before at the diner, so Annie didn't have to stand over a stove at home and spend a lot of time in the kitchen. The holiday menu consisted of ham, sweet potatoes, green beans, homemade bread and Jell-O salad with fruit. Annie fixed her famous iced tea and her delicious pecan pies.

Jonathan could only stay until noon because he had to catch a small airplane out of Herndon that would fly him to Memphis, where he'd board a larger airline that would take him to his grandmother's home in New York City. He was more excited about Christmas now, thanks to Annie and her children. Her house was decorated beautifully, and Annie never looked happier, he thought.

He had stopped by the diner the night before while she was cooking to give her a Christmas gift, but told her NOT to open it until New Year's Eve. That's when they were going to the Army base's annual New Year's Eve party for the employees and soldiers. A day before the party, Annie scheduled a hair appointment for a cut and curl at a hair salon in Herndon, and she couldn't wait to wear the sleek black dress and matching high heels that she found in a downtown boutique while Christmas shopping. All she needed now to complete the ensemble was a set of pearl earrings and a matching pearl necklace, so she subtly dropped a hint to Jonathan. When she saw his Christmas packages to her, she was pretty sure of what was inside them.

Annie lined up Lindy Sue to spend the night with her children on New Year's Eve because she did not plan to come home until the next day. Jonathan wanted her to spend the night with him at his home on Lake Wheatley. It was all she could think about for weeks.

Even though she was a successful businesswoman and mother, she still lacked confidence in a formal setting among dignified and educated people and had her "first adult-party jitters." But with Jonathan by her side, she was confident he'd have her back.

Dub was standing tall again and smelled better, too. On the day of their talk in her kitchen, Annie convinced him to let her buy his wrecker and ambulance service so he could pay bills and feed his animals.

"I don't want your vehicles, Dub," she said. "What I really want is my old Dub back, the sentimental and caring man that I adore. You won't take a handout, so let me buy them. You can buy them back from me when your business gets back on its feet. No one has to know except you and me. And I really don't care how long it takes you to pay me back, ya hear? Because it's not about money."

His head was low and his forehead almost touched the kitchen table. She reached under his chin and pulled his face up so their eyes could meet. His were red and swollen with tears. Her lips were slightly quivering, but she held onto her emotions for a few more sentences.

"It's about your self-worth, Dub. Right now, you are at the lowest point of self-worth that I have ever seen on you. And I want my old Dub back. The whole town needs you. Not just me."

He couldn't talk, so he just nodded in agreement. They both stood up and embraced across the table. Then they sat back down to talk about their personal relationship.

Through more tears and a few high-pitched words, Annie and Dub agreed that the two of them would be life-long friends, but not lovers. She told him about her love for Jonathan Shea, but he already knew it was strong.

"You are a good man, Dub Thomas," she said in a serious voice. "You will make some woman a wonderful husband. But we wouldn't work well as a married couple because you love me like a wife and I love you like we're kin."

He agreed. He loved her more than he had ever loved anyone in his life. He loved her kids, too, and would take a bullet for them. And no one had ever cared about him as much as Annie and her children. They were all the family he had in Cook.

"Just because I'm in love with Jonathan doesn't mean we can't be friends," she said. "It just means you can't pretend that I am going to change my mind and marry you. You need to get that out of your head. I love you as a brother, not a lover."

He was okay with that. Better a brother than nothing at all. He reached out and shook her hand to seal the deal. Then his mouth went in really close to hers and she pulled back.

"See?" she said angrily, pushing his body away. "That's exactly what I'm talking about, Dub! I just told you that I loved you like a brother, not a lover, and then you try to kiss me on my mouth. Brothers and sisters don't kiss there."

He started laughing. "Well ...."

She interrupted his reply, knowing full well where he was going next. "Well, nothing," she said. "I don't care what other families do, this is what our family does and it is the right way by the Lord. Understand?"

"Understand," he replied.

The transfer of Dub's property into her name was exhausting. Red flags went up and phones went unanswered everywhere she inquired. The holiday schedules and office closings of those involved put a kink in the deal, but Clyde stepped in and used his clout and business savvy to cut the red tape and acquire signatures from the authorities to give Annie the go-ahead.

She immediately contacted her sign man and hired him to paint advertisements on the garage windows for Dub's emergency services. The signs were not even dry before Dub got his first returning customer. The call came on Monday, a day before New Year's Eve. Starting the new year on solid footing was what both of them needed.

Lindy Sue arrived early in the afternoon on New Year's Eve to babysit and spend the night. Even though Jonathan wasn't picking Annie up until six o'clock, Annie wanted to take her time to dress and pack for her overnight stay with him, and she asked Lindy Sue to occupy her children while she pampered herself.

Earlier that morning she had washed and rolled her hair using large, bristle rollers like the hairdresser told her to do. The hairdresser also suggested Cutex's "Frosted Ice" nail polish for her hands and toes that she could purchase at the Woolworth's next door to the salon.

She shaved her legs and then painted her fingernails and toenails a frosted pink, hoping it was an appropriate color for a party with military people.

Around three o'clock, she poured a hot bath, sprinkled some of her Avon bubble bath into the water, and soaked until her fingers and toes wrinkled. She put on her blue Chenille robe, sat in front of her dresser, and applied her makeup by following the instructions and pictures in a *TEEN Magazine* spread. Then she removed the curlers and brushed her hair.

All the primping took so much time that before she knew it, it was almost time for Jonathan to pick her up! She doused her neck with a splash of "Charisma" by Avon, and then decided to spray a little on her upper thigh. Next, she stepped into her girdle and pulled it up to her waist. She carefully put her nylon stockings on one by one, affixing each of them to the girdle's garters. She took the tags off the dress, unzipped it, stepped into it, and pulled it up. She hollered to Lindy Sue to zip it.

"Oh, Mis' Annie!" Lindy Sue screamed. "You look like a movie star!"

Annie blushed. "Why, thank you, Lindy Sue. I feel like a princess, that's for sure."

"Well, your prince is going to be so happy when he sees you! You will be the most beautiful woman in the room. You'll see. And he will probably tell you that, too."

She heard his car pull up on the side of the house and Lindy Sue went to the front door to greet him. Annie found her shoes and put them on. They were wobbly on her feet, even though she had practiced walking in them a few times after she bought them. Her stomach did a turnover and she thought she was going to vomit, but she held it back. She looked through the crowded closet for the little black coat that Clyde's wife, Dora, let her borrow. Then she remembered it was hanging on the back porch to air out. She had to go through the kitchen to get to the back porch and she ran into Jonathan, who was getting a glass of water from the faucet. He almost dropped the glass when he saw her.

He blushed. She blushed. And then they both laughed nervously.

"Hi, handsome," she managed to say.

"Hi, beautiful," he answered. "You will … undoubtedly … be the most beautiful woman at the party," he said.

Annie smiled. "You know, Lindy Sue said you'd say that."

He looked into the living room at Lindy Sue and she winked at him. The children finished their TV show and joined in on the celebration of their mother looking so pretty.

"Oh, Mama! You are a fairy princess!" said Becky.

Dwayne said she looked like a movie star.

But Will was quiet.

"Will? Cat got your tongue?" she asked.

He shook his head. "No, Mama. You are the prettiest girl in the world. Are you leaving us and not coming home?"

Annie's mouth dropped. She walked over to Will and gathered up Becky and Dwayne for a group hug. "I will never leave you. Never. I don't ever want you to say it or think it or have nightmares about it! My life would not be worth living without you in it, do you hear me?"

All three of them said, 'Yes, Mama,' in unison.

Dwayne looked up at his mother with a serious face. "Mama, it is your turn to have some fun. Don't worry about me and Will and Becky. Lindy Sue will take good care of us and we got lots to watch on TV. Just be safe."

Annie was on the verge of tears but knew her makeup would run, so she took a deep breath and held them back from flowing down her cheeks. Jonathan put the coat around her shoulders and they walked out to his car. The kids stood in the doorway and waved goodbye.

Jonathan started the car up but didn't drive off right away. He put his hand on her left thigh and said, "Did you bring the Christmas gift I gave you?"

She stared into his handsome face and smiled, almost fainting with happiness. "Yes. Did you bring my gift for you?"

"Yes."

And in the car with only light from the moon and another from a 20-foot security light pole in the distance on the school's grounds, they opened their presents. She was right, he had listened to her and bought her pearl earrings and a matching string of pearls. She put them on in the car.

He opened his present and was happy to see black leather gloves and a beautiful key chain.

Then he said, "Would you like one more?"

She smiled and drew in a big breath and let it slowly release from her body. "Sure," she said softly.

"Well, do you think you can wait until after the party when we are at my house? Because I wouldn't want to mess up your makeup."

All she could think about was a tiny box with a diamond engagement ring inside. Her heart started palpitating and she was breathing rapidly.

"Yes, I can wait."

23
THE BONES

Sheriff Haynes was spending his New Year's Eve talking to two homicide investigators and a forensic specialist from Memphis who had come to Cook with results from the bones found under Pig Dog Diner's garage area.

They had determined that the approximate time of death was 15-20 years earlier, and that the bones belonged to an adolescent female. This female, they said, once had a broken right arm that did not heal properly.

The investigators wanted to know if there were any reports in Cook's police files about kidnappings or missing persons as far back as 1948 "or up until 1953," one of them said. Sheriff Haynes wasn't hired until 1955 and he didn't know the answer, but he said he would go through all the files.

The homicide investigator also wanted to know the history

of Tinkers Tow & Garage – who built it, who owned it, who operated the vehicles, and anything else he could find. The sheriff said he would have to talk to a woman named Dorthea Barton, the widow of the original owner, but he would start by talking to Mrs. Barton's daughter-in-law, Annie, who is the current owner.

"When you talk to the original owner, ask her about the names of everyone who worked for Tinker's Tow & Garage, and any owners other than her daughter-in-law," one of the investigators said.

"We have to look at all of these people as suspects. Someone with a wrecker or an ambulance has the opportunity to pick up people on the road, whether that's a hitchhiker, an injured person or a passenger of a towed vehicle. Both of these vehicles are suspect."

Sheriff Haynes was feeling sickly. Acid came up into his throat and he felt like puking. He was anxious to talk to Mama D, if he could find her, and to Dub and Annie.

The investigators started to leave the sheriff's office when they decided to tell him one more thing.

"By the way, sheriff," said the elder homicide investigator, "there will be an article in Friday's *Herndon Chronicle* about the bones. We asked that the writers give us a little more time to investigate before they write a story."

Sheriff Haynes was baffled. "How in the world did you pull that off? I can't believe they would "hold off" writing a story like this."

The investigator put on his cowboy hat and smiled back at the sheriff. "Yeah, you're right. But we told them if they ran the story, we would tell the Memphis paper about the piece of evidence we found with the bones. And if they wanted the exclusive, they'd have to wait. Thanks for your time, sir. I look forward to working with you on this case."

"You're welcome, sir," the sheriff replied. "I'll be in touch with you tomorrow afternoon and let you know what I find out. Could be that it may take until Thursday before I can reach all parties, but I will keep you posted one way or the other."

"Sounds great. Thanks. Have a good evening. And happy new year."

The sheriff paced around his office for a few minutes processing everything that was said. He kept trying to think of what kind of evidence could have survived for 15-20 years in a grave under the building. All he could think about was jewelry.

"Girls like to wear jewelry!" he said. "It's probably a ring. One that can be easily identified, like a birthstone with the owner's initials."

If that was true and the family of the female victim saw that ring in the newspaper, they would know it was their daughter's. His eyes were teary for the girl, her family, and the town of Cook that was about to be an injured party, too.

24
NEW YEAR'S SURPRISE

Annie rolled over on the soft white sheets and stretched her arms up high over her head. The sun was shining into the room from the large picture window that overlooked Lake Wheatley. She smelled the aroma of coffee perking in the kitchen, and knew any minute Jonathan would be returning with a tray filled with a morning brew and, perhaps, a pastry.

She rolled over onto her stomach and fluffed the pillow with her hands before plunging her face into the down feathers and smelling the sweet scent of vanilla. The blue satin teddy that Jonathan gave her when they arrived at his house after the New Year's party fit perfectly, and she marveled at his ability to guess her size so accurately. She remembered trying on the skimpy nightie for him while drinking a glass of bubbly, but she also remembered taking it off. She rolled over onto her back, smiled at the memories of their evening that were dancing around in her head, and waited for his return to the bedroom.

"You're awake!" he said, while walking into the room with a tray filled with food, coffee and a vase with a red rose. He set it down on the table near the bed and jumped into the cotton comforter to kiss her good morning. She turned her head.

"What are you doing!" she screamed, turning her head away from his face. "I can't kiss you without brushing my teeth first!"

He started laughing. Then he rolled over on his back and put his hands behind his head. "Okay, Miss Priss," he said sarcastically. "Go brush your teeth. But you'd better have them done by the time I count to 20 or I'm going to grab you up and throw you back down on this bed, bad breath and all!"

She hopped out of the bed and ran to the bathroom to get her toothbrush and toothpaste from her train case. She could hear him counting in the other room. By the time he got to 19, she was running toward the bed and jumped right into his arms.

He nuzzled his nose on her neck and could still smell her Charisma perfume from the night before. She began to moan softly. "Let's have some coffee, shall we?" he said in her ear.

Annie liked where the nuzzling was taking her, but agreed. "Yes, let's do!" she replied.

Jonathan poured each of them a cup of coffee and then began to take off the top of the sugar bowl when she politely declined.

"No sugar?" he asked.

"Nope," she said.

"Are you sure? Positively sure that you don't want any sugar? Because I think you might really like the sugar I have in my bowl."

Annie smiled. She liked it when he was playful. "Okay, you win. Give me some sugar. But not a lot, okay?"

He took the lid off the bowl and instead of white grains of sugar inside, Annie saw a small, blue velvet box with a tiny bow on it. Her eyes opened wide and she covered her open mouth with her hands.

He opened the velvet box slowly and revealed a beautiful diamond ring. "Miss Annie Barton, would you please be my wife?" he said, tears brewing in his eyes.

Her face was all scrunched up with tears and snot, uncombed hair and smeared eye makeup. She reached for a tissue next to the bed and blew her nose loudly.

Jonathan laughed. "Now, that's romantic!"

She was embarrassed, but managed to get some words out of her mouth. "No one has ever given me anything like this in my life," she said, sniffing and fighting back more tears. "And I have never loved any man like I love you, Jonathan."

"I love you, too, Annie," he said. "But you didn't answer my question."

Annie looked puzzled. "What?"

"My question!" he laughed. "Will you marry me?"

Annie felt like an idiot. "Yes. Yes, yes, yes!!" she said, jumping into his arms and almost falling off the bed onto the floor.

She held out her hand and he placed the ring on her finger. They were kissing themselves into another row in the hay when the phone rang and took their energy.

"Who could be calling me at this time of day?" he asked.

"Quick! Get it! It might be about my kids!" she shouted.

Jonathan picked up the receiver. "Hello, this is Doctor Jonathan Shea," he said.

A male voice answered back. "Doctor Shea, this is Sheriff Haynes in Cook. Sorry to disturb you on this holiday, sir, but I was wondering if Annie Barton was there with you."

Jonathan looked over at Annie. She stared back and shrugged her shoulder and mouthed, "What?"

"Yessir, Mis' Annie is here. Would you like to speak to her?"

"Yes," replied the sheriff.

Annie got up from the bed and walked over to the end table where the phone was. Jonathan handed her the receiver.

Her hands were shaking as she took the phone from him. "Hello, this is Annie Barton."

"Hello, Annie, it's Sheriff Haynes. Sorry to bother you. I got your number from Lindy Sue."

"What is it sheriff? Are my kids okay?" she said in a rushed, panicked voice.

"Oh, yes, they are just fine, Annie. I need to talk to you about something that has come up concerning your diner."

"My diner?" she asked, relieved. Jonathan's ears perked up like bird dog.

"Yes, ma'am, the diner. Those bones under the ground near the garage were female and had been there 15 to 20 years. The authorities want to talk to Mama D about them. Do you know how we can reach her? She ain't got no kin here anymore, so don't know who she's stayin' with."

Annie was rattled by the mere mention of that crazy woman's name. "No, sir, she left in a huff and I haven't seen her since. It was not a happy conversation."

"So she didn't mention where she was staying?" he asked.

"No, and I didn't ask," said Annie. "But she and Uncle Deek were pretty tight. He's about the only one in town that would put up with her. I'd check there first."

"Thank you, Annie, I appreciate yer help," said the sheriff.

"My pleasure, sheriff. Can I ask you a question, sir?"

"Well, I'll try to answer it, go ahead."

"Do you think she had something to do with killing that female?

"I can't answer that, hon," said the sheriff. "I just need to talk to her about the business side of Tinker's Tow & Garage. I know it belonged to Minner Brown and after he died it was sold to his Uncle James. Then James gave it to you and Robert in his will. I am investigating all the drivers of both of those vehicles that have been in your garage from as far back as 1948."

"Oh, I see," said Annie.

"How many drivers do you know about, Mis' Annie?" he asked. "Besides Minner and James?"

She was reluctant to answer and hesitated to collect her thoughts. "I'm sorry, what did you say, sheriff?"

He asked the question again. "How many drivers do you know of that drove the wrecker and ambulance besides Minner and his Uncle James?"

Annie felt faint with her reply. "Uh … well … I think … just one, sheriff."

"And who would that be?" he asked louder.

"Uh … that would be … Dub. He's the only one that I

know for both vehicles. But I could be wrong."

25
THE USUAL SUSPECTS

Sheriff Haynes knew it was New Year's Day and people would be hung over from partying all night, but the investigators were coming back in two days and he had to have some answers for them. Dub's farm was first on his list, and then he would visit Uncle Deek up in the hills.

He turned down the road leading to Dub's farm and hated like hell to have to talk to him about those bones. He knew Dub would take offense to it, and rightly so. But he also knew that he could lose his job if he didn't have some answers by Friday.

Dub's truck was backed up to the open doors of the barn and he was filling a stall with hay. He saw the sheriff's car drive onto his property and he threw the pitchfork into the truck's bed and began walking toward his police vehicle. He smiled and waved his hand. He removed his right glove to shake the sheriff's hand.

"Happy new year," sheriff," he said.

"Same to you, Dub."

"What brings ya all the way out here this morning?" he asked.

"It's business, Dub. Strictly business. And the more answers I get, the better I can fill out my report for the authorities."

Dub's ears perked up when he said the word "authorities."

"Sounds pretty serious, Larry. How can I help?"

"Well, you know Annie bought a storm shelter, right?" he asked.

Dub nodded his head. "Yeah, she's some kind of caring woman, ain't she? Said she wanted it for the community, too."

"Yes, she's a thoughtful person all right," the sheriff said. "But while they was digging under her diner in regards to that storm fixture, they found human bones."

Dub's mouth dropped. "Human bones? How do they know they ain't some dog or something?"

"Because they were collected and analyzed, Dub."

"Ain't that somethin'!" said Dub with a flushed face and a scowl. "What's that gotta do with me, Larry?"

"Now, don't get all in a hissy, Dub. I'm a sheriff and I'm just doing my job. Nobody is accusing you of anything, so don't go gettin' pissed off, okay?"

Dub just stared at the ground. "Okay," he said quietly. Then he looked up into the sheriff's eyes and said, "Don't know where this is going, Larry, and don't know who it's about, but I don't know nothin' about no bones under the diner's property."

The sheriff was happy to hear that, but he still had to get a statement from him. "I understand, Dub," he said, "but jest let me do my job, okay?"

"Okay, Larry," he said. "What do you want to know?"

"I need to know how long you've been driving for Tinker's Tow. And the names of any of the other drivers, too."

Dub thought a minute before he spoke. He squinted his eyes when he looked up toward the sky, like he was calculating something in his head. "I was 14 years old when Minner let me drive that wrecker the first time," he said. "I didn't have a license to drive until I was 'bout 18. I know that was wrong, but I never had a wreck or speeding ticket. No one knew 'cept Minner and Mama D."

The sheriff believed him, but needed to know more. "We are concentrating on the years of 1948 until 1953. Was there always a wrecker and ambulance service?"

"Minner had that wrecker when he opened Tinker's. That would have been about 1938. The ambulance was purchased from the Army base after them Army people purchased a new one. That mighta been 1939, because Minner died in 1940."

The sheriff was writing everything down on a little note pad. He stopped writing and looked up at Dub. "Okay, Dub, let's get back to the wrecker crew. Do you remember who could have been driving it from 1948 through 1953?"

Dub sighed and said, "Well, Uncle James was the owner, so he drove occasionally, but he was kinda sickly. Mama D helped with the books. She still had a hand in the business."

"Did she ever drive the wrecker?" asked the sheriff.

"Only in a pinch," he replied. "But Mama D knew all about vehicles of all kinds. Her granddaddy had a car lot and she grew up knowing a little bit about every kind there was. That Mama D was the boss of everybody, even after Minner died. Her husband, Jack, took all the calls that came in from outside of Cook proper, and I took all the local ones, but not until later."

"Okay, Dub, I think that's all I need to complete my report. If the investigators need more, I might be back to pick your brain some more. That okay with you?" he asked.

"Sure, sheriff, I don't see why not," he said.

The sheriff started to walk to his car when he remembered one more important thing. "I almost forgot to ask this, Dub, but is there a record log book of calls and their location anywhere?"

Dub thought a moment. "No, not a log that I know of. At least I never saw one. I just gave Mama D all my receipts. She may have kept a log. But I don't have any idee who would have them now."

Sheriff Haynes' head was swimming with ideas about the abduction of the young girl and who could have picked her up on the road and taken her back to Tinker's Tow & Garage where she was killed and buried under the garage floor of the wrecker's stall. His mind was reeling with all kinds of bad thoughts about Mama D and different scenarios involving her and Minner's Uncle James and Mama D's second husband, Daddy Jack. The men were both dead, so Mama D was going to be the next person he talked to.

Dub walked back to his barn to finish his chores, hoping he had passed the interrogation from Sheriff Haynes. He was a little nervous answering the questions because all he could think about was the missing metal box from Tinkers that he buried in the floor of an old tool shed along the creek behind the Wilks' house. The tool shed was gone now, and so was the box, thanks to the tornado. And the debris along the bank of the creek was removed by government workers.

It's probably in a landfill somewhere in the state, he thought. *No one will ever know what was inside.*

26
MAMA D GETS NASTY

Sheriff Haynes wasn't looking forward to meeting up with Mama D. There was a part of him that wanted to turn his police car around and go home, telling the investigators that she could not be located.

But the other part of him, the professional part, wouldn't let him do it. The professional in him wanted the woman to be located and prosecuted, if guilty. He had a gut feeling that Mama D knew something about those female bones.

As he approached Deek's homestead, he recognized Mama D's Buick from the day at the diner when she threatened Annie. He knew he was about to walk into something that wasn't going to be pretty. Mama D could be nasty. And Deek was nastier.

He banged on the door of Deek's shack and it opened right away. Mama D was staring him in the face. She let out a cackle like a witch.

"Lord have mercy, Deek!" she shouted. "It's Cook's Messiah!"

Deek came running out from the back room wearing just a dirty pair of drawers and nothing else. It appeared the lawman had caught the couple in the act of making love, but that couldn't be, he decided, because there was no love flowing in either of their veins.

"I'll just stay out here until y'all get a robe on or something," said the sheriff. "Holler when you got your clothes on."

Mama D started laughing. It was one of those laughs that chilled the sheriff's bones. A hateful, witch-like laugh from *The Wizard of Oz*, a movie he had just seen at the Erie Theater with his family.

She told him to come in or leave. Reluctantly, he entered their den of squalor. Both of them were smoking cigarettes and drinking whiskey, no doubt from Deek's still.

"Whadda you want, sheriff?" Deek asked.

The sheriff put on his professional voice and directed it at Mama D. "Dorthea, I'd like to talk to you alone, if Deek doesn't mind."

She looked over at Deek sitting in a big, oversized dirty

chair drinking his whiskey and smelling up the room with his cigar and body odor. He puffed out a string of smoke rings and said in his raspy voice, "Naw, y'all can go talk outside. This heer is my hause. You ain't got no warrant, sheriff."

The sheriff and Mama D walked out onto the front porch of Deek's shack. The air was better out there, anyway, the sheriff thought. He looked at the weathered woman and sighed. "What's got into you, Dorthea? Why are you back in town, and why are you with the likes of this loser?"

She started laughing. "Ain't any of yore business, Larry. What do you want from me? Spit it out or get goin'."

He frowned and she took offense to it.

"I said for you to spit it out, Larry, or I'm going inside. Either that or I smack that smirk off your face right here and you take me to jail. What's it gonna be?"

The sheriff took in a deep breath and let it exhale slowly. "Okay, Dorthea, we'll play it your way. We know about the bones that are buried under Tinker's garage."

Her eyes opened wide and her mouth flew open in a rage. "What are you talking about?" she screamed. "I don't know nothin' 'bout no bones buried thar. How dare you think I killed someone!"

Sheriff Haynes was getting tired of her nonsense and was a little hot under the collar, so he decided to go for the juggler. "I've got to turn in a report Friday to the investigators who have been working the case ever since the bones were unearthed a few months ago. The person was killed between 1948 and 1953, and the remains were found on the side of the garage where the wrecker is parked. Someone killed this person and buried the body there, and I mean to find out who that was. You can either talk to me or the Herndon police. Hell, you might even get arrested and get a square meal and shower out of it. It will probably be like going home to you, since you're kinda used to being behind bars now, aren't ya?"

Mama D didn't have any sarcastic comeback. She decided to cooperate so the sheriff would leave. "I don't know anythang 'bout that," she said in a somber tone. "After Minner died, I didn't do much for his uncle. I jest kept the books. But James, he was an odd one. Coulda been that old fart. I had to bail his ass outta jail many times and git the wrecker outta the impound yard lots of times. He's dead now, so thar ain't no proof of what I say. But I'd put my money on that bastard."

"What about Jack?" he asked. "I heard he helped with wrecker runs."

Mama D stiffened up at the sound of Jack's name. Tears formed in her eyes. "Don't be talkin' 'bout my Jack in that sense," she said. "He had trouble down there gettin' it up, know what I mean? It got to where he didn't want anything to do with no females at'tall. Not even Annie."

The sheriff was finished except for one last question. "Are there any records of trips made by the wrecker or the ambulance? Like a log book or receipts?"

Mama D began breathing harder. Sweat started dripping down her forehead. The sheriff knew he had hit a nerve.

"Naw, there ain't nothin' on my end. You should ask Dub 'bout that. That's all I got, Larry. Now git off Deek's property." She turned around and went inside.

The sheriff started walking toward his car. His head was spinning, trying to sum up the words from Mama D's mouth and her body language during the interrogation. Her response struck a nerve with him. He didn't say the bones were female. Why was Mama D talking about Daddy Jack's sexual disability?

He also had a gut feeling that she knew more than she was saying. After all his years in law enforcement, he knew when people were telling the truth and when they were lying. Sometimes, the pitch in their voice changes or they stop eye contact. They fiddle with things in their hands. They clear their throat. They sweat and breathe faster.

"Yep, she was lyin'," he said aloud as he drove away from Deek's shack. "She knows something for sure."

27
THE
INTERROGATION

New Year's Day is supposed to be a happy one, and everything was going extremely well with the newly engaged couple, Annie and Jonathan, until Sheriff Haynes called asking questions about Mama D's whereabouts in connection with the bones that were recovered from under the diner's garage.

Annie was anxious now to leave Jonathan's home in Lake Wheatley and return to her children in Cook. Just ten minutes earlier, she was dreaming about running away and eloping with the handsome doctor.

She wondered about her diner's reputation now that the bones had been identified as female, and how the newspaper would be all over it, just like they were after the tornado, calling Cook 'a haunting place to live.'

The reporters could say the same thing about my diner and Minner's tragic death, the female's death, and the hunt for a murderer, she thought.

Jonathan dropped Annie off in front of her house and she ran inside to her children. She gave Lindy Sue a ten-dollar bill for taking care of them overnight and offered to drive her home. But just minutes after Annie's arrival, Lindy Sue's father showed up at the door to escort his daughter home. Her daddy looked anxious and concerned.

"I know this ain't got nothin' to do with you, Mis' Annie, but I heard that bones were found under your diner's building," said Homer Smith, Lindy Sue's father.

"Yessir, they were, but the authorities say they had been there almost twenty years, long before I owned the place."

Homer seemed relieved to hear that. "I wondered 'bout that, Mis' Annie. Lindy Sue's maw and me, well, we ain't the gossipy type, but we heard the bones was someone fifteen or twenty years old."

Annie smiled. "Rumors can change from mouth-to-mouth," she said calmly. "The sheriff said the remains were *buried* fifteen to twenty years ago."

Homer seemed satisfied with that, but Annie knew that was not the end of the questioning she would receive from townsfolk and maybe even the press. She debated whether or not to open the diner or just wait another day. It was a holiday, after all. Nothing was open for business, so why should the diner?

Annie's telephone began ringing inside her house and she said her goodbyes and thanks to Homer and Lindy Sue. She ran back inside and saw Dwayne holding the receiver out to her.

"It's a newspaper man," Dwayne said. "He wants to talk to you, Mama."

Annie took a deep breath and reached for the phone. "Hello, this is Annie Barton. How can I help you?"

"Hello, Mrs. Barton, this is Tom Dawson at the *Herndon Chronicle*. How are you, today, ma'am?"

"I'm fine, just fine, sir, thank you," said Annie, her voice quivering a bit with anxiety.

"I'd like to talk with you about the bones that were discovered under the diner you own and operate in Cook. We got word today that they have been identified as female. We are running a front-page story about the bones in Friday morning's paper. Could we ask you a few questions regarding that discovery?"

Annie was shaking and hesitated to answer right away. What if she said something and it is interpreted wrong? What if the reporter doesn't quote her correctly? What if she doesn't know the answer?

"Mrs. Barton, are you there?" the reporter asked.

Annie took a deep breath. "Yes, I am here. What would

you like to know, Mr. Dawson?"

"Did you know the bones were buried there?" he asked.

"No, sir, I did not," she responded.

"Is it correct to say that the bones were found while a crew was digging around and under the garage area of your diner to install a storm cellar or bunker?"

"Yes, that is correct," she said.

"And the person who discovered the bones was Marty McKinnen, who was employed with Anderson & Sons Storm Cellars?"

"Yes," she replied.

"How well do you know Mr. McKinnen?" he asked.

Annie was taken by surprise and swallowed hard. She didn't know where the reporter was going, but all she could do was tell the truth. "I met Mr. McKinnen for the first time when he came into my diner to introduce himself after I had called his company, Anderson & Sons Storm Cellars."

"And he was there to meet you, Mrs. Barton? Or to assess the area where you wanted the cellar to be built?"

"Both," she said. "He is Clyde Tubbs' nephew. Clyde runs the store in Cook. Clyde wanted him to come in and introduce himself to me. I didn't know he was part of the Anderson & Sons crew until he came into my diner."

"And what did he tell you about the area where you were going to have a cellar built?"

Annie paused for about 15 seconds before answering. "He said that they were having difficulty with my storm bunker, and that they were going to have to dig closer to the foundation near the garage area. He was asking permission to do that. I said it was okay."

"How long was it before he told you there were human bones on the property and that they would have to shut down the day's digging?" he asked.

"Oh, right away," she said. "It couldn't have been more than 10 minutes. I remember him saying that he and his crew were waiting for the authorities to arrive and that they were coming right away while the dig was fresh, and before animals ran off with the bones."

"Very good, Mrs. Barton. Thank you for being so cooperative. I just have a few more questions. Is that okay?"

Annie sighed. No, it wasn't okay. She was tired of talking to this yahoo from the paper. But she agreed. "Okay. What else do you need to know?"

"Did Mr. Marty McKinnen mention any other items that were found with the bones?"

"What?" she blurted out. "Like what kind of other items?"

"Like ... specifically, jewelry," the reporter said.

"Jewelry?"

"Yes," he replied.

"No, he did not, sir. I know nothing about jewelry being found on my property," Annie said. "Mr. Dawson, are we finished talking now?"

"Just one more question, Mrs. Barton, please," he said.

"Okay," she reluctantly replied.

"Do you know anyone who is or was a member of the Masonic Lodge?"

"No, sir, I do not," she said.

"Thank you, Mrs. Barton. You have been very helpful. Have a good day."

"Thank you, sir," she said.

Mr. Dawson hung up on his end and Annie was shaking all over.

"What's the matter, Mama?" asked Becky. "You look so scared!"

Annie looked down into her baby girl's sweet face and smiled. "It's just grown-up stuff, hon," she said. "Go get your brothers and let's all sit down in the living room. I have some exciting news to tell y'all."

Becky ran to get her brothers and all three were seated on

the couch when Annie walked in. They motioned for her to sit in the big, fluffy chair. They had big grins on their faces.

"We know, Mama," said Will.

Becky hit his arm with her elbow. "Will!! You spoiled the surprise!! Don't mind him, Mama. Go ahead, tell us."

How could the kids know about her engagement ring unless Jonathan had told them? He must have asked their permission first, then sworn them to secrecy. She pretended not to know about their inside information. She reached into her pocket and pulled out a beautiful diamond ring and slipped it over her ring finger on her left hand. Then she held it up in the air for them to see. The children oohed and aahed, but they weren't genuine.

They were fake.

"Y'all already knew, right?" Annie asked.

All three said, "Nooooooo, Mama!"

Then, all four of them cracked up and ran to their mama for hugs and kisses.

"We love Doctor Shea," said Will.

"Yeah, Mama," said Dwayne.

"He will be the best daddy," said Becky. "And he will be good to you, Mama. You deserve to have someone be good to you."

28

THE EVIDENCE

Annie awoke early Friday morning to someone pounding on her front door. She grabbed her robe from the foot of her bed and wrapped it around her body as she walked toward the door. She peeked through the window to see who it was, and was surprised to see Marty. She opened the door slowly.

"What's going on, Marty?" she asked. "Is everything okay?"

"No, it ain't," said Marty angrily, pushing the door wide open and entering her living room. "Who gave you the right to talk about me and my business to the newspaper people?" he yelled, shoving the front-page of the *Herndon Chronicle* up into her face.

Annie stared at the newspaper's lead story and lost her ability to speak. Someone had taken a picture of her diner and blown it up to cover half the left side of the page. To the right of

the photo was the story and headline: "CLUES TO COOK
DINER MURDER EXPOSED." A photo below the story showed
a necklace and a small, round pin with a logo on it, two pieces of
evidence that were discovered with the female bones under the
garage of her diner.

She sat down on the couch in the living room and felt like
she was going to faint. Not because Marty was mad or that her
diner was being depicted as a murderous scene.

Annie was upset because she recognized one of the items
found with the bones.

Marty was pacing around Annie and breathing heavily
when Sheriff Haynes showed up. Annie looked up into the sheriff's
eyes and tears trickled down each cheek.

"Oh, good, the sheriff is here," said Marty. "Arrest her,
sheriff, for quoting me and using my last name without giving me
so much as a heads-up that the press had talked to her."

"Now, now, wait a minute, Marty," said Sheriff Haynes. "I
read the story, too, and Annie here didn't say anything that
incriminated you in the crime. She simply told the reporter how the
bones were found and answered honestly about who found them.
No one thinks you had a hand in this cover-up, Marty. You're out
of line here, son."

Marty's face was beet red with anger. "Never in all my
years of excavating suspicious items from peoples' yards and under
their houses has someone mentioned me in a newspaper article,
sheriff. Wouldn't you be upset if you arrested someone and they

talked about you in the paper for all the world to see?"

Sheriff Haynes threw up his hand and said, "I can't tell you how many times my name has been in the paper, son," he replied. "It comes with the territory. No one is going to think you had a hand in something like this when the forensics people said the bones had been buried 15-20 years ago. Why, you were just a pup back then."

Marty put on his baseball cap and started walking toward the door. "If I do get fired or get any kind of threats, Annie, I'll be seeing you in court." He turned to walk toward the door when Annie piped up.

"I had no idea you were so mean-spirited, Marty," she said. "I can't have that kind of negativity living next door to me and my children. I lived with that kind of attitude and meanness for far too long. You need to look for another house to rent because mine is not available to you anymore."

Marty's face was filled with rage. "My Uncle Clyde won't take too kindly to this news," he said. "You'll be sorry."

Annie let out a little laugh, which irritated him more. "You should strive to be more like your uncle, Marty. Why, Clyde is the most kind and just person I know. He will see beyond this stupid accusation you've made and see the truth. What happened to that guy who said to me, 'This isn't my first bones discovery?' How do I know that YOU didn't plant them there? Maybe that's what I should have said to the newspaper reporter. But I didn't. I told the truth. And if that truth hurts, then you need to change your line of business."

The sheriff was enjoying the bantering between Annie and Marty. "Here, here, you two. It's not against the law to tell a newspaper reporter what another person said, unless that person didn't say it and it is a lie. Was what she said in the newspaper a lie, Marty?"

"No, sir. It wasn't."

"Then I think this is just a situation that is unfortunate for you and Annie and this community. Bones were found, they were analyzed as female, and the jewelry probably belongs to the victim. That's a good thing, to have a piece of jewelry that someone can identify as their daughter's or their sister's. Now, the pin is a little different because there are so many of those pins in existence. So, Marty, you finding these bones may answer some questions for loved ones of this female."

"You're right, sheriff," he said. "And I'm sorry, Mis' Annie. I got this hot head and sometimes I say the wrong things."

Annie smiled and looked him in the eyes. "I know people make mistakes about other people's intentions, but my intentions were good. You were just mean to me, Marty."

"Will you accept my apology?" Marty asked.

"Yes," replied Annie. "But you're still not renting my house."

Marty turned and stormed out the door, leaving Annie and the sheriff in the living room. She could see her kids standing in the door of the kitchen, and motioned for them to go back to their rooms.

The sheriff started to leave and Annie stopped him. "Wait a minute, Larry," she said. "I have one more thing to say."

"There's no reason to say anything else, Mis' Annie. I read the paper and I think you answered all the questions fairly. Marty had no call to talk to you like that. He used to be a hotheaded guy in his youth. I thought he left all that behind him."

"It's not about Marty," she said, calmly. "It's about the necklace that was found. I saw the picture of it on the front-page. You're right about someone recognizing it as a loved one's jewelry."

"Yeah, we don't always have items like that to go on," the sheriff said. "So you think you might know about this girl? How could you know about a girl that died when you were …. maybe three years old?"

"Because I think she is my cousin, Lurleen."

29
ANNIE'S TURN TO SPEAK

After reading the Friday edition of the *Herndon Chronicle*, verifying with Annie how she had knowledge of the owner of the necklace, and concluding his interviews with Dub and Mama D, Sheriff Haynes made a call to one of the homicide investigators in Memphis.

That evening, the investigators were in Herndon at the police station where the sheriff agreed to meet. They had already talked to Lurleen's family, who confirmed that their daughter, indeed, had a broken right arm that was not tended to by a physician, and Lurleen's mother described the necklace that once belonged to her own mother. There was no doubt in anyone's mind that the bones and the necklace belonged to Lurleen Smith.

Now it was Annie's turn to meet with them, and she was happy to oblige. In a tiny room with no pictures or windows – just a table and four chairs – Annie told the detectives what they had already heard from Lurleen's parents, how Lurleen went missing, the circumstances around her abduction, and the shrine in her aunt's home with a portrait of her daughter wearing the necklace that was found on her diner's property along with her bones.

The detectives wanted to know more about Lurleen's family, and Annie couldn't really tell them.

"I just now got acquainted with them, sir," she told one of the detectives. "It happened when my Uncle Titus died and my kids and I attended his funeral. They were long, lost relatives until then, but I'm sure they will be happy to know that their daughter's remains have been found so they can bury her properly."

The detectives seemed okay with that, but they still needed more from Annie. Detective Jim Cardwell took the lead.

"You know we have to look in every nook and cranny, at every human associated with her, and consider every situation," he said. "What was your observation of this family at the funeral?"

Annie thought for a moment, but wasn't quite sure what he was fishing for. "What do you mean, sir?" she asked politely.

The detective took a deep breath and exhaled through his nose, which Annie perceived as frustration. He put on a condescending smile and said curtly, "I don't know how to say it any clearer than that, Mrs. Barton. Just tell us about these people."

His attitude stuck in her craw. She looked him straight in the eyes and said, "If you want my help with this case, you have to be more clear with your wording."

The detective pushed his chair back, stood up and walked around the room. He lit a cigarette and sat back down and faced Annie. This time, though, he was more precise and polite.

"Okay, Mrs. Barton, you win," he said arrogantly. "What we are looking for with this family are any devious or jealous people, perhaps someone with a criminal background or someone who might have said something about the girl being a troublemaker or an older male who likes young girls. Was there a family member who didn't fit in well? Did everyone get along? You know, anything suspicious with anyone or any situation? Hell! I don't know!"

"You don't have to raise your voice, sir. I will tell you what I observed. I saw a loving family who has been grieving over their daughter for 15 years, a family who has turned their daughter's bedroom into a shrine. My impression was love. They loved their daughter, and discovering that her bones have been buried under the diner's foundation all these years has probably started their grieving all over again. I think they were hoping to find her alive. I think that is what has sustained them all these years. But I don't understand what their family has to do with this. It appears that she was picked up in a vehicle or a wrecker and taken back to Tinker's Tow to be buried. How could you possibly think it is someone in her family who did this? Did someone in her family work for Tinker's Tow back then? I am so confused!"

"We have to look at everyone, Mrs. Barton. It might sound

like a long shot to you, but we are looking for any connections, too. Whose funeral did you attend?" the detective asked nicely.

"It was Lurleen's uncle's funeral."

"What kind of guy was he? Did you get a feel for him?"

"Well, sir, to be truthful, yes. Yes, I did. Lurleen's mother told me he was a bigot. In fact, they were not sad that he had died. My Aunt Myrtle said he had meanness in his bones and caused a lot of pain for everyone."

The detective seemed happy with that and scribbled it all down on a piece of paper. "Do you know if your Uncle Titus was a Freemason?"

"No, I do not know what that is," she answered.

"What can you tell us about Dub Thomas?" he asked.

Annie was taken aback. She sat up straight and asked, "Dub Thomas? Why do you want to know anything about him?"

"Well," the detective said, "he was one of the wrecker drivers during the time that the deceased went missing. Mr. Thomas would have driven the wrecker into that garage and parked it in the very same place that the bones were found. That's why. So tell us, what do you know about him?"

"I know him very well," she said, "and my children do, too. He is not related to me, but I consider him a family member. He has helped me and my children when we were going through some dark times. He is loving and giving. Everyone loves Dub."

"I see," said the detective. "Is this the same loving and giving guy that you were about to stab one day with a kitchen knife?"

Annie started to cry. The only way the detective would know about that incident was from Marty. "Yessir, he's the one. I must tell you that …"

The detective cut her off. "No need to explain, Mrs. Barton. We have a pretty good feel for Mr. Thomas, thank you. We'd like to know more about your former in-laws, Jack and Dorthea Barton. And their son, your former husband."

Annie felt heat rising up her throat and into her head. She despised those three people and no matter how hard she prayed, the hate never went away. She was quick and direct of her assessment of the Bartons.

"I was a prisoner in their home, Detective Cardwell. I was treated like a slave and mistreated in a number of ways. I do not wish to talk about those vile people. I will never, ever forget my horrible years with them. But I thank God every day for the three beautiful children that resulted in that arranged marriage, children that I love and adore with all my heart."

"My apologies, Mrs. Barton, but I had to ask. Your late father-in-law was also a wrecker driver for Tinker's Tow, and your former mother-in-law was also involved in the business when Lurleen Smith went missing."

"Yes, I understand that you have a job to do," she said through quivering lips and weepy eyes.

"Just one more thing, Mrs. Barton," the detective said. "Was your father-in-law a Freemason?"

"I have no idea," she replied. "What does that have to do with anything? Why are people always asking that?"

"Sorry, ma'am, I can't answer that right now," the detective said. "Thank you for coming in today. Sorry we got off to a rocky start. We'll be in touch."

"Your apology is accepted," she said as she walked out the door. "I hope you find the bastard who did this to that sweet young girl."

"I hope so, too," he replied.

30
WINTER WOES

January 1969

Tennessee weather forecasters in the upper west portion of the state were predicting the coldest month on record for January. Snow was falling every day, schools were closed, mail routes were delayed but, somehow, someway, Cleo and Harlan delivered the *Herndon Chronicle* to Clyde's store in their brand new 1969 Ford F100 using their snow plow attachment on its shiny new grill.

Schoolchildren were happy to be home the first week. They slept late, watched TV, played board games, and created lots of snowmen and snow creatures. Then boredom began to sink in the second week.

Annie was lucky to have a job within walking distance of

her home. Her children came with her to help out because Henry was stuck in The Bottoms with no way out. The rickety bridge from his house to the diner was piled with snow and drooping in the middle from the weight. County workers were risking their lives scooping up the snow across the bridge with shovels, only to have it all covered with more snow the next day. But each day the workers shoveled it because an accumulation over several days would snap the bridge in two.

Clyde lived in a two-story home next to his store, so he was open early and stayed late. When he first heard the weather forecast, he stocked up on coffee, milk, bread, cereal, lunchmeat, canned soup, crackers, potted meat and more. Before the snow began to accumulate, a lot of residents drove to Herndon with their Styrofoam coolers and bought meat.

Annie wasn't able to see Jonathan. Because of the long drive from Lake Wheatley to the Army base, he slept in one of the barracks there. They talked daily and missed each other madly, but safety was their number one concern. The nightly news was all about the weather, the traffic deaths, the dangerous and slick roads, and furnaces that couldn't keep up with the cold.

Many of the children who had to stay home from school were sledding and playing outside in the elements. Consequently, they got hurt or fell sick with colds and fever. The visiting doctor from Herndon, who came on Mondays and Thursdays, was stuck in Herndon, creating a hardship for those who were ill in Cook. Clyde was taking the brunt of everyone's complaints about not having a full-time doctor. There hadn't been one since Doc Wilks, and he died five years earlier. So Clyde decided to approach Cook's powerful ten movers-and-shakers and suggest they consider hiring a full-time doctor. Cook's mayor, George Wilson, brought it up at the Cook City Council Meeting that meets monthly at the school, and it was passed. One of the council members had a grandson who nearly died from lack of proper medical attention, and that's all they needed to vote "yea" all around.

Annie heard about the vote while making pancakes one morning in the diner. A few of the council members and their friends were talking loudly over their breakfast and she overheard them discussing the pros and cons of hiring a full-time doctor. Annie jumped right into the conversation.

"More coffee?" she asked while visiting their table with a pot of fresh brew in her hand. "I couldn't help but overhear y'all talking about a new doctor in town. Is it true? Are we going to get one soon?"

"Yep, it appears so, Mis' Annie," said Councilman Duane Bixby. "You gonna get your fella to apply?"

"Well, I guess that would all depend on the salary. The Army pays him pretty nicely. Have any numbers been thrown out there yet?"

The four men looked around the table at each other, whispering, smiling and nodding. Mr. Bixby looked up and answered her question. "Have your future husband give me a call. Here, take this napkin. I wrote my phone number down on it. If he's interested, I think we could work something out."

Annie couldn't wait to tell Jonathan. When he called later that day, she didn't tell him about it at first. She asked him how his day was going and if they were treating him with the respect that he deserves.

"No, Annie, they are not," he said. "I think they forget that I was head of a department at a hospital. Either that or my position is not really a priority for the Army right now. Our presence in Viet Nam is where their minds and hearts are, and I have no desire to join the Army and go over there as a medic."

Those were exactly the words Annie wanted to hear from Jonathan's mouth. "And I wouldn't want you to go anywhere," she replied. "What would we do without you, Jonathan?"

"I know, sweet girl," he said in his kind voice. "This really is a good job. It's stable and pays well. It has perks and benefits. We are lucky that I have it. I wouldn't be able to afford my house without this job."

He was right. It *was* stable. She liked that a lot, considering she was engaged to marry him! As her husband, he would have to cloth and feed four more people, and the Army wasn't going anywhere. But what happens when the Viet Nam war ends? What will happen to that base? She just had to tell him about the new job opening up in Cook.

"I am so proud of you, Jonathan, but have you ever thought of having your own practice?"

"Yes," he said immediately. "Why? Is that what you want me to do? I haven't brought it up because we'd have to move out of Cook and that wouldn't work at all. So I'm stuck here for a while until maybe something opens up in Herndon. But those doctors over there are like bloodhounds. They sniff out the ones they want to be included in their medical offices and it is getting so bureaucratic."

Those words were music to Annie's ears. "Well, guess what?" she asked.

"What?" he replied. "Is this a game we're playing or is this a real thing we're doing here?"

"No, it's for real," she said. "What if I told you that the Cook City Council is about to approve funds to pay a resident doctor?"

"Well, the first thing that comes to mind is 'how much would the City Council control that doctor?' Because city councils don't normally do things like that. Did someone tell you they were considering hiring a doctor?"

"Yep, I overheard it in the diner."

There was no hesitation in Jonathan's reply. "Well, I am interested in being that doctor, but I am not interested in receiving money to do it. I would set up my own practice and run it like my own business, not the City of Cook's. Tell me more about what they said."

A few new customers came into the diner and she asked him to hold on a minute. When she returned to the phone, it was a dial tone. She hung up the phone and called him back. He answered right away.

"Sorry I had to hang up," he said. "My supervisor walked by and I am not allowed to have personal calls while on duty."

"See? All the more reason for you to have your own practice, Jonathan," she said. "You wouldn't have a supervisor looking down your throat. There is a need in this town and you have a need inside you to help people. Won't you consider branching out on your own? Doc Wilks didn't have a problem making a living at it! Everyone loved that old man. All I ask is that you think about it. If you have to sell your house and I have to sell some land, let's do it! Let's invest in our future!!"

"I've got to get back to work now, Annie, and I will think about everything you said, baby," he replied. "I would love all that to happen."

"Okay, but just hear me out for one more second. What if that City Council brought in a doctor who wasn't competent? And Becky got sick and he gave her the wrong medicine and she died?"

"Oh, hon, I don't even want to think about that! But I will really give this a lot of thought, okay? And I really have to go now. I'll talk to you later, baby. I love you so much."

"I love you more," she replied.

31
THE CALL

February brought drier weather, higher temperatures and roads that were passable. Life got back to its normal state in Cook, but old wounds slowly began to surface. Investigators continued to question residents about people who worked in some capacity or another at Tinker's Tow & Garage during the time that Lurleen Smith went missing – particularly Mama D, Daddy Jack, Dub, and Uncle James. Two of those potential killers were dead, and only Mama D and Dub could answer for them.

"One of them knows how Lurleen Smith's bones got under that garage," said Lem Smithers. "They had their hand in the pot and knew who was stirrin' it."

Residents took bets on who it would be.

The one piece of evidence that was lacking – and crucial – was the logbook, the paper trail that would determine the day the call came in and the time and place of the tow that took that wrecker to the vicinity of where Lurleen would have been hitchhiking. It had not surfaced and the police were frustrated. That is, until they got a telephone call one morning from someone with a muffled voice. It was difficult to determine if the voice was male or female or young or old because the person was speaking through a towel or washcloth. But what the person said was incriminating.

"This heer is for Detective Cardwell," the voice said. "Y'all need to look at Dub's hog pen."

It was the first tip that had come into the police station regarding Lurleen Smith's murder. The Herndon detectives were all pumped up about digging up the hog pen on Dub Thomas' farm, and their minds went haywire thinking about what could be hidden there. The logbook? More bones? Buried evidence of other murders? Money? They were out of control and rabid.

They quickly phoned the Memphis homicide detectives to let them know about the message to Cardwell. The Memphis team was baffled that the detective's name was given. That meant only one thing to them at that moment: the person who left the muffled message was someone close to a person who was interrogated by the Memphis investigators, particularly Detective Cardwell, and that name alone linked the caller to the Lurleen Smith case.

The Herndon police received the go-ahead to file for a search warrant posthaste, but they had a difficult time convincing the Herndon Police Chief that the call was, indeed, related to Lurleen's death in some way.

After a heated consultation and lots of convincing, the chief agreed that they could file for a search warrant to dig up Dub's hog pen for evidence that "might be linked to a homicide." It was granted immediately, and the team of police investigators headed to Dub's farm with all their forensic equipment and digging tools. The policemen were acting like bloodhounds, channeling their olfactory bulbs and anxious to track their prey.

Dub had just left the diner and was turning his truck onto the road toward his farm when he saw numerous police vehicles and trucks ahead of him. He followed them all the way, wondering where they were going and who was in trouble now. When they turned onto his property, his heart began to beat rapidly, his brow dripped with sweat and he almost peed his pants.

He watched them from afar as they ran to his front door with their guns pointed. They started yelling for him, and when he did not answer, they began to break down his door. That's when he got out of his truck and walked toward them. One of the officers saw him approaching and turned to face Dub with his gun pointed at his chest.

An officer recognized Dub from a black and white photo he was shown before he left the station. "On the ground! On the ground!" the officer shouted at Dub.

Dub put both hands up in the air. "What's going ...."

"On the ground! "Get on the ground" another office shouted.

Dub reluctantly got down on the ground. Two officers

walked toward him. "Put your hands behind your back now!" one of them screamed.

Dub did as he was told. They cuffed his wrists behind his back and yanked him up to his feet by pulling up on his right arm. He squirmed to get the officer's hand off his arm. The officer shoved him forward. They read him his Miranda Rights. One of them thrust the search warrant up into his face. He read it as fast as he could before the man stuffed it back into his suitcase.

He chose to be silent while watching the officers drag their gear toward his hog pen and start digging. His clothing wasn't warm enough to stay out in the cool weather, so he asked if he could sit in a squad car. They said 'no,' so he sat on the ground with his back up against one of front tires of a vehicle, which shielded the wind from his body. He didn't have a good view of the pen from where he sat, so he couldn't see what they were retrieving from the mire.

Four hours later, a freezing Dub was placed in the back of one of the police vehicles and transported to the Herndon jail. He was fingerprinted, photographed, showered and clothed in a jail uniform and placed in a cell by himself. He was allowed to make one telephone call and dialed Annie's number at the diner.

"Pig Dog Diner, this is Annie speaking."

"Hey, girl, it's Dub."

"Hey, Dub."

"I'm in the Herndon jail."

Annie gasped, sucking in lots of air down her throat. "What? You're in jail?"

Customers' heads turned in the diner when they heard her say 'jail.' She moved around the corner into the kitchen out of earshot.

"What are you doing in jail?" she whispered.

Dub's end was silent. Then she heard him moan. "I don't rightly know, Annie," he whispered. "The police were diggin' on my property for somethang. They cuffed me, made me sit out in the cold for hours, and now I'm heer in this gall dern jail wearin' jail duds."

"What can I do, Dub? Do I call a lawyer? It's awfully late, though. I know, let me call the sheriff and see what he has to say and we will do everything we can to get you out and get to the bottom of this!"

"Okay, Annie, thank you," he said. "They haven't been very nice to me in here, either. They are treating me like a criminal."

Annie hung up the phone and called Sheriff Haynes. He didn't know what was going on and said he was going to drive to Herndon to find out. Annie wanted to go with him, so she called Lindy Sue to sit with the children and stay the night. She also called Jonathan to let him know what was going on and that she would be gone several hours and not to worry. Jonathan was not at all happy about her leaving the children at night and going to rescue Dub. But he knew that Dub was like family to her, so he took in a deep breath and said, "Give Dub my best, hon."

They reached Herndon about nine o'clock and almost everyone was gone except the officer out front. He couldn't answer any questions that the sheriff asked, only confirming that there was a Dub Thomas in custody, but no visitors were allowed. Sheriff Haynes got on the phone to the Herndon mayor, who was married to his mother's cousin, and the mayor said he'd call him back.

Annie and Sheriff Haynes drank black coffee and waited in a small area in front of the check-in desk for two hours before the mayor called back. The night clerk received the call and handed the phone over to the sheriff.

"Well, Larry," the mayor said, "it looks like we might have us a murderer behind bars. It ain't been verified, but Herndon police got a tip about investigating Mr. Thomas' hog pen, and they found some bones that looked human."

The sheriff held the phone tightly to his ear so Annie couldn't hear the mayor's loud voice. She sat looking up at him with a concerned face all the while he talked.

The mayor said there wasn't anything that could be done tonight and told them to go home and come back tomorrow. "But in the meantime, find a lawyer for the bastard," he said.

32
WALTER J.
BRISCOE

Annie spent all evening calling around to see if anyone could recommend a lawyer for Dub. She didn't want just anyone, though. He had to be someone who had years of experience, particularly a criminal defense attorney who specialized in homicide. She wasn't having any luck and it was getting late. At 10:30 p.m., she decided to wait until morning to finish her calls.

She tossed and turned in the bed and couldn't fall asleep thinking about humans being eaten alive by Dub's hogs. Eventually, she dozed off and dreamed about a young girl being thrown into the hog waller and chomped on by the swine. The only thing left of her were her teeth floating atop the runny yuck and gunk.

Her eyes opened wide and she sat up quickly in the bed with sweat dripping down her face and tears running down her cheeks. She cried for thirty minutes, wondering how many bodies the detectives thought were buried there. She tried to go back to sleep, but her nose was stuffed up and her eyes ached. Finally, the alarm clock went off and she rose from her night of horror, blood, guts and body parts.

Jonathan was waiting for her outside the diner and had a huge grin on his face. He couldn't wait for her to open the door.

"What?" she said, smiling, as she put the key into the lock. "What's going on? What do you know that I don't? And what are you dying to tell me?"

He just kept smiling and nuzzling the back of her neck.

Once inside, he swung her around to face him and planted a big kiss on her mouth. She moaned with contentment and fell limp. "Okay, okay, don't tell me then," she said returning his kisses. "I'm perfectly fine remaining in this state and not hearing what you're holding inside you."

He pulled away from her face a bit. She could smell the sweetness of his morning mouthwash as he began to talk.

"I got a hold of my college buddy, Walt, and he has agreed to take Dub's case."

Annie's mouth opened wide and then broke into a huge grin. She threw her arms around his neck and kissed his cheek, his ear, his neck and then his mouth. "That is the best news! When is he coming?"

"Tomorrow. He has his own plane and is flying into Herndon around four. He'll be staying at my house for a few days, but then he said he'll be moving to a motel near the courthouse. He said the residents of Herndon don't have any idea what's about to hit them. We're talking national news, newspaper reporters from all over the U.S., an increase in the city's crime, maybe some rioting."

Annie made them both a cup of coffee and they sat in the booth and talked. "Tell me more about Walt, hon," she said.

Jonathan took a sip from his cup and looked up at the ceiling. "See that roof on your diner?" he asked.

Annie looked up. "Yep, why?"

"Because Walt's background, reputation and courtroom presence is taller than that. He is one hellava guy, in and out of the courtroom. Everyone should be afraid of what he's going to turn up. He knows where all the bodies are buried."

"What?" Annie asked. "What bodies?"

He laughed and reached out to caress her cheek with his hand. "That's just a saying, sweet girl. It just means there's no hiding anything from this guy. If he can't get Dub freed, no one can."

All the talk about Walt got both of them hungry, so Annie fried up some bacon and scrambled eggs. They ate them like they hadn't eaten in days.

"See?" Jonathan said. "His energy is already affecting us and you haven't even met him yet!"

He was right. She was famished. "I don't understand! Why am I so hungry all of a sudden?"

"It's your endorphins," he said. "Those chemicals that your body releases when you have feelings of excitement or sexual attraction or even when you smell your favorite food. Having Walt in town is an endorphin rush!"

She held up her coffee for a toast. "I'll drink to that!" she said.

They both laughed.

God, he loved her. She was his endorphin rush. He watched her interact with customers who entered the restaurant for breakfast. She hugged everyone like they were related to her and they hugged her back. No wonder they ate there! She brought on their appetite!

He held up his hand and signaled for her to come to his table. He had to leave for work, but he really didn't want to go anywhere without her along. She came over to his table and said, "That'll be three thousand dollars."

He laughed. "Wow, why the discount today?" he asked.

She tried to hold back a smile and said seriously, "Because you didn't order toast."

He stood up and pulled her to his chest. He didn't care if

anyone was watching. They were engaged, for gosh sakes!! He held her and then kissed her forehead. She didn't want him to leave and held him tightly.

"You know that you have to let me go, right?" he asked.

"Yeah, I know. But I needed just a little bit more," she said.

He wanted more, too, but his boss would be all up in his face if he was late. But if he was his own boss, he could've stayed another hour. Annie's suggestion about starting his own medical practice in Cook was sounding better and better each day.

Jonathan worked until almost three o'clock and then left the base to pick up Walt at the Herndon Airport. He stood in the terminal and watched Walt land his 1968 Cessna 310N TURBO jet on the runway and then taxi over to the gate where he was greeted by airport personnel who were wheeling out metal stairs for deplaning. Walt opened the door of the cockpit and walked down the stairs holding his briefcase in one hand and a cigar in the other hand. Jonathan hardly recognized him.

Walt began walking toward the terminal and spotted Jonathan inside. He put his right hand up in the air and waved. Jonathan waved back. He hadn't seen Walt in more than 10 years, and by the size of him, it was 100 pounds ago, too. He was massive, a good 250 pounds with a gut that hung over his belt. His once brunette hair was now gray and pulled back into a ponytail, calling more attention to his matching gray beard. His silver rings adorned all eight fingers, and a silver bolo tie held a jade pendant.

He looked more like a pirate than a lawyer. All that was missing was a black patch over this right eye and a peg leg.

"How are you, you old son-of-a-bitch?" he said, man-hugging Jonathan and pounding his back with his massive hands.

Jonathan pulled away from Walt and looked him in the face. "I almost didn't recognize you, Walt! Where'd all that grey hair come from? You're only 38!"

Walt puffed on his cigar and then let out a hearty laugh. "Three ex-wives, alimony, child support, these damn cigars and no sex, that's where," he said.

Everyone in the small airport thought Walt was a movie star. "My mom wants to know if you are somebody important," asked a young boy about 10.

"You go back and tell your mother I am *very* important," he said.

The boy ran back and told his mother and she just smiled and waved.

"I have that effect on women now," he said to Jonathan. "They just smile and wave at me now. There was a time when they were sexually attracted to me. Now it's my wallet they're in love with."

"Same old Walt," Jonathan said. "I can't wait to show you around."

"First, I have to meet this fiancée of yours," he said. "It's

Annie, right?"

"Yes," said Jonathan. "We'll stop at her diner on the way to my house in Lake Wheatley. She can't wait to meet you."

"Likewise," said Walt.

On the way to the diner, Walt asked a million questions about the community, Annie's diner, the garage attached to her diner, Dub Thomas and the previous owners of Tinker's Tow. Jonathan told him what he knew, but he told Walt that Annie would be able to supply him with all the answers.

It was now six o'clock and dinner was in full swing at Pig Dog Diner. Walt and Jonathan got lucky and found a perfect table near the front window, and Annie waved from the kitchen when she saw them come through the door. She was nervous meeting Walt. Jonathan painted a "larger than life portrait" in her brain of the man who was going to represent Dub, and she is always intimidated around smart people. She slipped into her shy mode, but fought it hard.

"How can I help you gentlemen tonight?" she said, putting menus in front of the two men.

Jonathan looked up and said, "Well, first, I'd like you to meet Walter J. Briscoe, attorney at law."

Walt rose from his chair and kissed Annie's hand when she extended it for a shake.

"How do you do, Mr. Briscoe," she replied.

"Aw, call me Walt," he said.

Jonathan rose from his chair and kissed her on the forehead. "Hey, beautiful. What's on the menu tonight?"

Both men sat down and listened to Annie rattled off all that was available to eat and drink. They both settled for fried catfish, fries, slaw and iced tea.

"Good choice," she said. "And we have pecan pie and ice cream for dessert."

"We'll take it all," said Walt. "And won't you please join us afterward?"

"Why, I'd be happy to, sir," she replied.

The whole time that Jonathan and Walt were in the restaurant she was sick to her stomach. She knew that Walt was going to want to talk about Dub. *"How did she know him? "Did she think he was capable of killing another human being?" "Had she been to his farm and seen his hog pen?"* And other questions that she was not crazy about answering. But she would tell the truth, whatever he asked. And she decided not to do it at the diner.

Annie asked Henry if he would close up the diner so she could take Jonathan and Walt to her house for coffee and to meet the children. He said yes, and they all arrived at her house about eight o'clock. Lindy Sue had the kids bathed and in their pajamas when they arrived. They stayed up fifteen minutes before they were shooed to their beds.

At the kitchen table, the three adults drank more coffee

and talked another two hours. When Walt asked if there was anyone else who knew about Dub and his past, she didn't lie.

"Yessir," she replied, "Mr. Clyde Tubbs who owns the grocery store. He knows about his past. He is a very nice man who will probably be very helpful to you."

33
THE TRIAL, DAY 1

News travels fast in small rural communities. Everyone was gossiping about the fast-talking attorney that was causing havoc in the court building in downtown Herndon. The cartoon in the *Herndon Chronicle* depicted Defense Attorney Walter J. Briscoe as a Gladiator and the District Attorney Kenneth Moody as Don Knotts' character, Mr. Limpet, because he was a slight man who wore a fedora hat and round glasses.

The cartoon caption read: "David and Goliath to battle it out in Herndon court."

Trial was scheduled to start in a week. Witnesses were being summoned and a jury was on the docket for the next day to select the men and women who would decide the fate of Dub

Thomas.

Annie was one of those who received a summons to appear in court on the opening day of the trial, which was Monday, March 17, Saint Patrick's Day. Of course, the *Chronicle* cartoonists had another field day with that date, this time with leprechauns. They drew a small cartoon figure of D.A. Moody with a beard and a pipe in his mouth, and Briscoe as a giant of a fella asking for a handout from the D.A.'s pot of gold.

Annie was nervous about testifying. She was familiar with a courtroom, but only vicariously through the television show *Perry Mason*, so she knew a little about what to expect. But the show never had a man like Dub as one of its actors, and never was there a crime involving human bones in a hog waller.

She couldn't decide what to wear or how to comb her hair. Should she wear a dress or a skirt and blouse? *A dress.* Hosiery? *Absolutely.* High heels or flats? *Heels.* Hair up in a French twist or down and loose around her shoulders? *No, a ponytail. No, not a ponytail, that's too youngish. A French twist.*

"I just need to be myself," she said aloud. "I will wear what I wore to church last Sunday. If it's good enough for church, it's good enough for the courtroom." The weather was still pretty cool for March, so she wore the long-sleeved navy dress with its navy and white striped collar and matching belt, black pumps and a short, lightweight black coat. She bought the complete ensemble from the Sears Catalog, so the outfit should be appropriate, she thought. Depending on how long the trial would last, the wardrobe of many key players would change when the weather decided to turn to spring-like temperatures.

She wondered how Dub was holding up and if he liked his larger-than-life attorney. Surely, he would see the value in Walt and his background as a criminal defense attorney and feel more confident. But when Dub walked into the courtroom, Annie nearly fainted when she saw his shaved head, skinny body and pale face. She held back tears that she knew would make her start bawling uncontrollably. Instead, she dabbed her eyes with her hankie and took in several deep breaths.

The bailiff entered the courtroom and called the court to order, then the judge entered and every person in the room was on their feet.

"Everyone but the jury please be seated," the judge said.

Then the bailiff asked the jurors to raise their right hands so they could get sworn in. After that was done, the judge looked at the prosecution and asked the District Attorney, Kenneth Moody, to stand and begin his opening statement.

Listening to the D.A. made Annie very, very angry.

"Your Honor and members of the esteemed jury, you are about to hear testimony in a case that is both horrifying and barbaric ... a case concerning the discovery of the bones of two unidentified female bodies that were thrown into a hog pen and devoured by swine, and the bones of a third victim found in the ground under the Pig Dog Diner garage. Whether they were dead or alive when cast in their graves, we do not know."

D.A. Moody paused and walked over to Dub, pointed his finger at him, and continued his opening remarks. "On trial today is this man, Dub Thomas, who owned that hog pen, the man who had the means of meeting and transporting the victims to the pen through a service vehicle of his employer, and parked his vehicle in a garage where the bones of an identified female was found. We intend to show how the defendant planned and executed each murder with malice forethought. We also intend to prove that both grave sites of these three women – the hog pen and the defunct Tinker's Tow & Garage – are connected to one killer, and that the alleged guilty party is Mr. Thomas who is responsible for both crime scenes."

Then he walked over to his seat and sat down. The judge looked at Walt. "It is now time for the defense to deliver its opening statement."

Every eye in the room followed Walt's impressive and exaggerated form rise from his chair and face the judge. "Thank you, your honor," he said. Then he turned to face the jury members, who were mesmerized by his image of strength, intellect and power. He was like a superhero that had been summoned to save the world from destruction, and they were all under his hypnotic spell. He delivered his flawless opening statement with the composure of a preacher in a pulpit.

"As members of the jury, I don't have to remind you that a man is innocent until proven guilty in this wonderful nation of ours. Nor do I have to remind you that there must be evidence to support a verdict of murder, and that hearsay and gossip is not evidence.

We will prove to you that the defendant is innocent of the crimes he is accused of, and that others in his town of Cook, Tennessee, had access to his farmland where the hog pen is located, and access to the area of Tinker's Tow & Garage where the third victim was buried. There are no witnesses that claim to have seen the defendant in the company of women who have gone missing, nor are their witnesses that saw the defendant depositing the human bodies in either place. There are no witnesses that claim he confided in them and admitted committing such crimes, and there is no record of the defendant being anything but a fine, upstanding member of his community.

But I just want you to think of one simple thing while listening to the testimonies in this courtroom – just one simple thing that will put everything into perspective: Anyone on this earth can wrongfully accuse another of committing a crime, and it's their word against the other. That's why we have a court of law. And just because your neighbor keeps his curtains closed on his windows 24 hours a day doesn't mean something bad is going on inside. Because your neighbor could just be blind."

He turned and walked back to his seat. There was an eerie silence like God had spoken. People began to fidget in their chairs and the judge sensed it. He banged his gavel.

"Will the prosecution call its first witness?"

D.A. Moody stood up. "The prosecution calls Mrs. Annie Barton to the stand, your honor."

The bailiff walked forward to swear Annie in. "Please raise your hand. Do you solemnly swear to tell the truth, the whole truth and nothing but the truth so help you God?"

"Yes," she said.

"Please be seated."

Annie walked over to the witness stand and sat down. She was fidgeting with her handkerchief in her lap. It helped calm her nerves.

"Good morning, Mrs. Barton," the D.A. said.

"Good morning," Annie replied.

"How long have you known the defendant, Mr. Dub Thomas?" he asked.

"Well, probably since I was about twelve years old," she replied.

"Probably?"

"Yes, I was twelve."

"And what was your first impression of Mr. Thomas?" he asked.

"Well, I remember thinking that he could do just about anything. He could fish, hunt, pull people out of ditches with his truck, run townsfolk to the hospital in his ambulance and feed the workers at the cotton gin. He was a very nice man."

"I see," said the D.A. "What is his relationship to you now?"

"He is a good friend."

"Oh, really? Just a good friend?"

"OBJECTION!" shouted Walt. "Argumentative."

"Objection sustained," the judge said.

"Mrs. Barton, how would you describe his temperament?"

"OBJECTION!" Walt shouted. "Misleading."

"Objection overruled. The witness may answer the question," said the judge.

Annie was getting frazzled. All the shouting and tension just didn't settle well with her. She started shaking inside and her hands were trembling. "What was the question again?" she asked.

"How would you describe his temperament?" the D.A. asked.

"Well, I would have to say he's normal. He is on the road a lot and has to take care of a lot of people, plus he has his farm and all his chores. He has a lot of responsibility and I think he handles it well. His temperament is normal, I think."

"I see," said the D.A. "Would you say that having to defend yourself against the defendant by wielding a knife at him normal behavior?"

"OBJECTION!" yelled Walt. "Inflammatory!"

"Objection sustained," said the judge.

"Your honor, I have no more questions for this witness," said the frustrated D.A., who wasn't at all happy with Annie's answers, but at least he got to plant a seed for the jurors about Dub's anger issues.

Walt was up next. You could hear a pin drop when he rose from his chair. "Mrs. Barton? May I call you Mrs. Barton? Or do you prefer Annie?" he asked.

She smiled and said, "Mrs. Barton is just fine, sir."

"Have you ever been to Mr. Thomas' farm?" he asked.

"Yessir, on numerous occasions."

"And why would you have gone to his farm?"

"He has a wonderful apple orchard and he lets me pick apples for my pies that I make and serve at my diner."

"Very well," said Walt. "Any other reason you would be out there?"

"No sir."

"When was the last time you saw Mr. Thomas?" Walt asked.

"Before he was arrested, I would see him every day," she said. "He parks his emergency vehicles in the garage I own that is next to the diner. He pays a rental fee to use the garage. I guess you could say we are business partners."

"So, let me get this straight so the jury understands. You and Dub Thomas are just friends."

"Yessir."

"How does your family feel about him?" Walt asked.

Her voice lighted and was more expressive. "Oh, my children love Dub," she replied. "He is a part of our family. When my children and I were living with my late husband's parents in an abusive household, Dub was my champion. He helped me deal with the abuse by being caring and supportive. He was my only friend then, and I just don't know what I would have done without him!"

Annie's words caused Dub to tear up. She had to stop her testimony to cry into her handkerchief. A few of the jurors were wiping their eyes, too.

Walt continued his questioning. "So Dub's a good guy."

"Yessir, the best," she said, sniffling. "He's the reason I have a diner. When I was able to escape from the clutches of the Barton family, Dub got all the townspeople together for a big dinner in the mart area of Tinker's Tow & Garage. I had inherited Tinker's when my husband, Robert, died, and Dub thought it would make a great place for people to come together and eat. He proved that, too. He asked about 40 townsfolk to bring dishes of food to Tinker's and they set up card tables inside the mart like a restaurant. All of them, not just Dub, helped make Pig Dog Diner a reality. Yes, Dub's a good guy."

Walt was smiling. The jury was smiling. They all thought Dub was a good guy. But Walt had to ask just one more question that he hoped the judge would approve if the D.A. objected to it.

"In your opinion, Mrs. Barton, do you think Dub Thomas is capable of killing another human being and throwing their body into a hog pen?"

"OBJECTION!" shouted the D.A. "Leading the witness!"

"Objection overruled," said the judge. "You may answer the question, Mrs. Barton."

"No sir, I don't. Dub couldn't even put his dog down when it had grown so old it couldn't walk. He had to get someone to shoot his horse when it broke both of its front legs trying to jump over the creek. No, the Dub I know and love as a friend could never do that to a human being."

"No more questions, your honor," said Walt.

The jury smiled. But just as the prosecution was about to call its next witness, the electricity went out and people could not even see their hands in front of their faces. The judge hollered for everyone to stay still and not to move because they would hurt themselves. In about five minutes that seemed like thirty, three men came through the door with flashlights and walked everyone out to the street. But before they got up, the judge struck his gavel on the hard wood of his bench.

"Court will reconvene tomorrow at 9 a.m. when we have adequate lighting," he said.

Annie was glad it was over for her, but she knew Clyde's testimony could undo all the good she had just spoken about Dub. Not that Clyde would do it on purpose. He cared about Dub, too. But he knew Dub's background and it wasn't a pretty picture.

What concerned her most wasn't that Dub's brother and sister took their own lives.

It was when Clyde told her that Dub would go missing from time to time.

34
THE TRIAL, DAY 2

Annie tossed and turned in bed all night and didn't drift off to sleep until about 4 a.m., only to be awakened two hours later by the loud alarm clock. She threw back the covers and hurriedly walked down the hall to the bathroom to draw her bath.

She was happy that Henry was taking care of the diner during the week of the trial, and grateful for her brother, Buddy, who was helping in the kitchen, and Lindy Sue, who got the children dressed and walked them to and from school each day. Her stomach was giving her fits, but it always did when she was nervous about something. She blamed it on the courtroom and the uncertainty of Dub's future.

As soon as she pulled her truck up onto the highway to

Herndon, she noticed more traffic than usual. As a result, the speed was slower and it took almost 45 minutes to reach the courthouse.

Were they all going to the trial? Walt said the national news would carry the story and reporters and spectators would come just to be a part of it.

She couldn't find a parking spot out front and had to park a block away, which meant she had to run to the courthouse before the doors closed and locked. Out of breath and weary, Annie sat down in the first spot she saw that was large enough on the bench seats to fit her butt. A hand reached over and grabbed hers. She jerked it back and looked up. Her eyes met Jonathan Shea's. He was sitting next to her! She smiled and rested her head on his shoulder. He kissed the hair on the top of her head and stroked her arm, which eased her anxiety. She sat upright and took a deep breath, exhaled it slowly, and was now ready for whatever the day was going to bring.

Annie turned her head toward the jury box. There appeared to have been a few substitutions overnight, and she wondered if that was normal. She counted three new faces and nudged Jonathan. He leaned his left ear toward her mouth.

"I think there are three new people on the jury," she whispered.

"Shhhhh! Keep your voice down!" a woman behind her said.

Annie sat up straight with her eyes forward. Jonathan squeezed her hand. She looked around the courtroom and saw a packed house, mostly female. The trial hadn't even started and many spectators were fanning themselves from the heat generated from all the bodies in the room and the numerous perfume odors.

Almost all of the ladies in the jury and half of the female spectators were wearing their Sunday best, and about a quarter of them looked like hussies. It was then that Annie began to see the impact that the defense attorney was having on those in the courtroom.

It was the endorphin rush that Jonathan told her about, and it was present and in the form of Walter J. Briscoe.

Before the judge allowed the attorneys to begin calling their witnesses, he made a small announcement.

"Overnight, we were told that three female jurors had fallen ill and have been replaced with three alternates from the jury pool."

Annie wondered if the husbands of those three ex-jurors had something to say about their wives' "swooning" over Walt. And, just as Annie had suspected, Clyde Tubbs was the first to be called to the witness stand.

"Mr. Tubbs," said D.A. Moody, "how well do you know the defendant?"

Clyde looked over at Dub sitting across the room. "I have known him most of his life, sir."

"In what capacity?" the D.A. asked.

"Well, I run the grocery store in Cook and Dub was a

young boy when he came to work at Tinker's Tow & Garage, which is a stone's throw from my store."

"Who was running Tinker's Tow & Garage at the time Dub Thomas was hired?" the D.A. asked.

"Mr. James Smith," Clyde replied. "The original owner, Minner Brown, died in a car accident in 1940, and his Uncle James brought the place soon after."

"I see," said the D.A. "And what did Mr. Thomas do for Mr. Smith?"

"Dub drove the wrecker," answered Clyde.

"And how old was he when he began driving the wrecker?" the D.A. asked.

"I think he was 'bout fourteen."

"What about the ambulance?" asked the D.A.

"Well, I don't believe Dub was qualified to drive the ambulance at such a young age. I think he mainly drove the wrecker until he got older and more mature," Clyde said.

"Do you recall any other people working at Tinker's Tow & Garage driving the wrecker besides Dub and Mr. Smith?"

"Yessir. Mr. Brown's widow, Dorthea. She kept the books and filled in occasionally behind the wheel of the wrecker and the ambulance, and there was also Mr. Brown's friend, Jack Barton, who helped out, too."

"Barton? Please tell the court if Jack Barton is related to Annie Barton who testified yesterday," the D.A. asked.

Clyde seemed a little irritated having to link Annie to the scoundrel Jack Barton, but he was under oath and had to comply. "The late Jack Barton was Annie Barton's father-in-law. He married Dorthea Brown after her husband, Minner Brown, was killed in a car accident."

"I see," said the D.A. "So besides Dub Thomas, there were three other people who drove the wrecker."

"No," replied Clyde, "there were four."

Several spectators gasped loudly, inhaling suddenly at the sound of four possible suspects.

The judge sounded his gavel. "Order in the court!" he yelled. "Mr. Tubbs, you may continue now."

"Thank you, your honor," said Clyde. "Minner's Uncle James was another driver, but not for long. He had some disease that made his hands shake, so he ran the business from home base. Dub eventually drove both vehicles, and Jack filled in as a driver. Dorthea was responsible for the books, but she could also drive that wrecker in a pinch."

The D.A. had a smirk on his face. "That's a lot to take in, Mr. Tubbs. We may have to draw a diagram of these people and their relationships to each other for the jury to get a firm grasp about who they are and what they were responsible for doing and who they were related to. I'm sure it's confusing to some people who are just hearing their names and relationships to each other for the first time."

"That it is," said Clyde. "A diagram would be a good thing."

"Mr. Tubbs, let's get back to Dub Thomas. Has he ever been married?"

Clyde thought for a moment. "No sir, not to my recollection."

"Any girlfriends?"

"No, sir, I do not believe he has had a girlfriend, but we don't talk about those things, you know?"

"No, I don't know, Mr. Tubbs. Cook is a small town and you don't know if Dub Thomas had a girlfriend?"

"I can honestly say that I have no recollection of Mr. Thomas having a girlfriend," Clyde said abruptly.

"What can you tell the court about his past?" asked the D.A.

Clyde's patience was wearing thin with the D.A. "His past what?" he asked.

"You know, what can you tell us about his family and where he came from and how he came to be in Cook. Was he born there? Did his parents raise him there? Did he have any siblings?"

Clyde took a folded handkerchief out of his back jean's

pocket and wiped his forehead that was wet with perspiration. "He lives on a farm that once belonged to his adopted parents. When they passed, the biological children, which was an older brother and sister, ran the farm. When they both died, Dub inherited the property.

"Is that all, Mr. Tubbs?" the D.A. asked.

"Yes," replied Clyde.

The attorney was wearing a smirk on his face like he knew something about Dub that Clyde knew, also, but Clyde wasn't saying any more. The D.A.'s face became distorted with an annoying smug look. "What can you tell us about Mr. Thomas' parents?"

Clyde knew what the attorney was fishing for and he wasn't sure if he wanted to go on record with hearsay about Dub's biological parents. He looked over at Dub and saw him put his hands over his ears. "I did not know the family well, sir. They kept to themselves," Clyde answered.

The attorney was getting cocky now. He knew he had hit a panic button. He knew this was his Perry Mason moment. He walked around the courtroom and stood in front of the jury with his hand on the railing. He looked at the jurors and then turned his head toward Clyde. "Isn't it true, Mr. Tubbs, that his mother and father were actually the brother and sister?"

Almost every mouth in the courtroom inhaled suddenly from astonishment and many began to choke and wheeze while catching their breath.

Walt wasted no time and yelled, "OBJECTION, YOUR HONOR!! HERESAY! THERE IS NO PROOF THAT MR. THOMAS IS A VICTIM OF INCEST."

The judge beat his gavel. "Objection overruled!" the judge said. "Proceed, Mr. Moody."

Dub's head was on the table resting on his arms. Walt was whispering in his ear to sit up straight and face the devil before him who was disguising himself as the district attorney.

"Mr. Tubbs, I will ask you again," said the D.A. "Isn't it true that his parents were actually brother and sister?"

Clyde was pissed. Hot air was coming out of his nostrils. "There is no record on file at City Hall that states that Dub's parents were siblings. In fact, you can …"

Clyde's testimony was interrupted by a female voice.

"I AM DUB'S MOTHER," shouted a woman from the back of the courtroom. "He is my son and I gave him to the Thomas family because they wanted another child. Mis' Ethelyn Gibbs delivered him."

All eyes looked at the frail woman standing before the sea of spectators and legal team. Annie couldn't believe her eyes, mainly because she didn't think the woman was old enough to be Dub's mother and, secondly, because she thought it was a hoax.

The whole courtroom erupted and people got up out of their seats and were getting kind of rowdy. Walt stood up and everyone quieted, waiting for the true master of the room to speak.

"Your honor, if it pleases the court, I believe we have a new witness to swear in today," Walt said calmly, turning toward the woman.

The D.A. was speechless but managed to dismiss Clyde, but not without telling him that he may be called again at a later time. The bailiff was asked to swear in the skinny woman who walked shakily to the stand and held up her right hand and vowed before God and a courtroom of confused people that she would tell the truth. She sat down in the witness chair and began to weep, and blew her nose into a small hankie.

The D.A. could barely speak. He cleared his throat and said, "Please state your full name for the record," he asked.

She looked out at the crowded room of serious faces and her body started teetering like she was about to faint. But somehow she managed to utter the words everyone was dying to hear.

"My name is Verneice Annette Stokes."

The entire courtroom erupted into chaos. Someone threw a woman's shoe in the direction of witness stand and someone else blew a whistle. It was like a three-ring circus had come to town and Verneice was the main attraction.

The judge hit his gavel numerous times before everyone calmed down to hear her testimony. And just like that, it was so quiet you could hear a mouse squeak.

The D.A. was not prepared for the witness. He did not know who Verneice was, but he didn't let on that he was in the dark.

"How would you like to be referred to in court? Miss or Mrs.?" the D.A. asked.

Right away, Walt knew he had no idea who Verneice Stokes was. He nudged Dub with his right elbow.

"It's *Miss* Stokes," she replied to the D.A.

"And how do you know the defendant, Dub Thomas?"

Verneice looked over at Dub, who had picked his head up from the table and was smiling at her. She smiled back, waved, and pointed at Dub. "That handsome man thar is my son, Dub."

"Your honor, if it pleases the court, we would like to proceed with a cross-examination of this witness," the D.A. said.

The judge hit his gavel and said, "Proceed, Mr. Moody."

Walt was trying to hold back his joy.

"Thank you, sir," he replied. "Miss Stokes, can you explain to us how Dub became a member of the Thomas household if he is your son like you said he is?"

"OBJECTION, YOUR HONOR! ARGUMENTATIVE! MISS STOKES ISN'T ON TRIAL HERE. IS THE D.A. CALLING HER A LIAR?" shouted Walt.

The courtroom started buzzing and the judge had to silence them with his gavel. "Objection sustained," said the judge. "Mr. Moody, please ask your question again to Miss Stokes."

"Yes, your Honor," he replied. "Miss Stokes, when was Dub born and how did he become a member of the Thomas household?"

Verneice brushed back the hair from her face and tilted her face upward toward the crowd. Channeling her Norma Desmond character from the 1950 movie *Sunset Boulevard*, she opened her eyes wide like she was ready for her close up. "I was just thirteen when Dub was born. My mama made me give him up to the Thomas family. He never knew."

"How old are you, Miss Stokes?" the D.A. asked.

She smiled and her voice took on a flirty tone. "Why, Mr. D.A., don't you know it ain't polite to ask a woman her age?"

The judge struck the gavel and she jumped in her seat on the witness stand. "The witness will answer the question truthfully," the judge said.

Again, the D.A. asked Verneice her age.

She hesitated again. "I am 47, sir."

"And how old is Dub Thomas?" he asked.

She looked over at Dub and he was still smiling at her. "He's only 34, but he thinks he's 37," she said in a playful way in her Southern Belle accent. "I had a deal with the Thomas's that they would lie to Dub about his age so it didn't come back and ruin my fine reputation," she said.

Walt and Dub were trying to hold back their laughter. The

courtroom was whispering and some were chuckling and the judge had to reel them in with the gavel.

"ORDER!" he said twice. "Will council please approach the bench?"

Walt and the D.A. walked over to the judge. In a low, but stern voice, the judge told them to "get this circus act together" or he would file a contempt of court. The two lawyers agreed.

The D.A. spoke first. "Your honor, I have no further questions for this witness."

The judge looked over at Walt. "Mr. Briscoe," the judge said.

Walt's massive presence took over the room. "Thank you, your honor," he said. He walked over to the witness stand and looked Verneice in the eyes. She was swooning all over him. He knew he had her in the palm of his hand.

"Miss Stokes …"

She interrupted. "You can call me Verneice," she said, fluttering her eyelashes.

The courtroom erupted in laughter. The judge hit the gavel again, several times.

"No, Miss Stokes, you are in a court of law now and we have protocol," he said. "I will be calling you Miss Stokes and not your first name. Is that clear?"

"Yessir," she said, smiling.

"Okay, so now that we have determined that Dub's parents aren't his adoptive brother and sister or from the planet Mars, can you tell us who his father is and how he came into this world without going to a hospital and obtaining a medical record?"

Verneice looked over at Dub and winked. Then she blew him a kiss. Many in the courtroom sighed. Then she began her story.

"Well, I can tell you that Cook's black midwife, Ethelyn Gibbs, delivered my baby boy and my mama took him right over to the Thomas's. They named him Delbert, but everyone called him Dub. When he was about three, Mr. and Mrs. Thomas died in a head-on collision on their way back from a funeral in Memphis. That's when the two older children, who were in their late teens, raised Dub on that farm until he was 18. Then they all got a sickness that took their lives, except Dub's! Me and my mama heard that it was scarlet fever, and we prayed that Dub would be spared and he was! But those Thomas siblings taught Dub everything they could about growing apples, raising hogs, milking cows. He could do everything! He started driving the farm's truck and plows when he was about ten. When the Thomas siblings died, Dub's name was on the will and he inherited everything."

You could have heard a pin drop all the time that Verneice was talking. Everyone was so engrossed in her story and Dub's story and the Thomas family that many knew nothing about prior to that day. But there was only one thing she neglected to say, and Walt called her down on it.

"Miss Stokes, thank you for being so informative about Dub's past, but you did not tell us who Dub's father is."

Verneice looked around the room to see if he was still there, but he was gone. She had decided to announce the identity of Dub's father to the jury only if he was still in the courtroom so he would have to fess up to it in front of TV cameras and newspaper reporters in the lobby, because he had sex with her without her consent. When her own mother confronted him about her daughter's pregnancy, he put all the blame on Verneice.

Verneice looked over at the judge. "Do I have to tell everyone who Dub's father is? Would that make any difference? Can't I have some time with Dub first?" she pleaded.

The judge liked her for some reason. Maybe because she was so brutally honest.

"Yes, ma'am, you can," the judge said. Then he hit the gavel and said, "Court is adjourned for today and will resume tomorrow morning."

The TV crew, newspaper reporters and radio personalities pounced on Verneice as soon as she walked through the doors of the courtroom. But Walt stepped in and guarded her like a giant from a Golden Book story. He fought off the journalists and walked her to a back room with no windows and asked her to stay there for a moment.

"Don't answer this door unless you hear three consecutive knocks," Walt instructed Verneice.

Then he returned to the courtroom and asked the bailiff to bring Dub by to see his mother. The bailiff refused. "I'll cuff her, too, if you're worried about her exchanging something between them," said Walt.

But the bailiff changed his mind when Walt talked him into a one-minute exchange of hugs between mother and son.

Walt and Verneice were waiting by the door when they heard a slight rap. Walt opened it immediately and saw Dub with his arms cuffed behind his back. He was ushered inside out of sight and Verneice hugged and kissed his face. He cried like a baby.

"Oh, Dub! I am so sorry for not telling you that you were my son! Can you ever forgive me?"

She pulled away and looked in his face. He had tears flowing down his cheeks, but he was smiling.

"I knew we had some kind of connection," he said. "Now I am just wondering who my dad is."

She hugged him tightly again as the bailiff was pulling him away. "It's Clyde Tubbs," she whispered in his ear.

"Clyde's your daddy."

35

JONATHAN'S PLANS

After an emotional and exhausting day, Annie asked Jonathan to stay overnight and take her to court the next day. Seeing Verneice and hearing her testify under oath that she was Dub's mother was confusing to Annie. If it was the truth, which she was pretty sure it was, then everything that Clyde told her about Dub's upbringing was some kind of cover-up.

It was all she could talk about, and she and Jonathan were still discussing it when they got into bed. Annie was baffled. "But why would Clyde make up a story about Dub being a product of incest, given to a brothel, then found in an abandoned box car and taken in by Pete Bilbow? What motive did Clyde possibly have for telling a whopper of a lie like that?" she asked Jonathan.

He shrugged his shoulders. "I don't know, sweet girl. Maybe he's Dub's father."

Annie's eyes opened wide and a big grin spread across her face. "That's got to be it!" she cried, jumping up and climbing on top of him in the bed. "He's got to be the father! And did you notice that Clyde was missing when the trial was over for the day?"

"No, I didn't," said Jonathan. "Guess he'll take his retirement off the back burner now."

"Or maybe it will be sooner," she said. They both laughed, only it wasn't that funny. Annie rolled off him and onto her side of the bed, looking up at the ceiling while lying on her back.

"I wonder if his wife, Dora, knew," she said. "I bet she didn't. Can you imagine what kind of turmoil is going on in their house right now if this is true? Because if Clyde kept it secret all these years, he's got to tell his wife now. He's not stupid. Verneice is back and it will come out for sure. Dora is probably crying herself to sleep and their phone is ringing off the wall. This town is never going to be the same after this scandal. I can just feel it!"

Jonathan was tired and he still had some news to share with Annie. "Can we talk about something else right now?" he asked nicely.

"Sure," said Annie. "What's going on?"

He turned toward her and placed his right elbow on the pillow and propped his head up with his hand. "Well, I'm just going to blurt it out there for you," he said, avoiding her eyes and

245

fidgeting with the lace bow on her nightgown.

Annie propped her head up on the pillow in the same manner and got face-to-face with her husband-to-be. "Okay … blurt away!"

He took in a deep breath and said, "I quit my job at the Army base and I am going to see about opening my own medical practice in Cook."

Annie leaped toward Jonathan from her side of the bed and straddled her legs around his middle torso. She bent down and kissed him passionately on the lips and then came up for air.

"I am so happy!!" she cried. "That's the best news! Finally! Something good to talk about! Tell me your plans – tell me, tell me, tell me!"

Jonathan was smiling ear to ear. He was excited, too, about having his own practice and being his own boss. "There's only one thing I want to happen before we open the doors to the clinic."

"What, hon? Tell me and I'll do what I can to help you!" she said excitedly.

"Oh, you can help me, all right," he said. "I want us to be married."

She was still sitting on top of him in the bed and bent down with tears in her eyes to kiss his lips. "I would love that, too!"

Then she thought about the trial. "I hope this trial doesn't drag on for months. It's just mid-March. Surely it will be over by June. I would love to have a June wedding."

"Me, too," he said. "And we can go ahead and get the clinic ready for patients. That's not a problem. I just want you to be my wife when it opens. You are going to be such a wonderful doctor's wife. Any ideas for the wedding?"

Annie rolled her eyes and smiled. He knew something big was coming by her look. "I want you to wear a tuxedo with a top hat," she said. "And I am going to wear a beautiful white flowing gown."

He threw back his head and laughed. "A tuxedo with a top hat?"

She nodded her head 'yes.'

"Do they even make them anymore? I mean, didn't that go out of style like in the forties?"

She rolled off him over to her side of the bed and stared up at the ceiling. She folded her hands and laid them across her chest and said softly, "When I was a prisoner in the Barton house I would visit the creek every morning to bathe the stench from my body of those horrible Barton men."

He reached over to pull her into her arms, but she didn't budge. "No, just let me finish, okay? Because this is important to me."

"Okay, hon," he said, lying back down on his side of the bed and staring at her beautiful face.

"Well, I found a page from a movie star magazine one day while bathing in the creek, and it had pictures of a man in a top hat and tails dancing with a woman in a white flowing dress. They were both smiling and happy to be alive, and I just knew their life was filled with nice words, pretty music, a white two-story home and a big fancy car. I imagined him stopping every now and then and whispering, 'I love you, Annie Louise.' "

Jonathan reached over and pulled her into his arms. "That's a beautiful story, one that I know helped you through your dark days. And if you want me to wear a top hat and tails, then I am happy to do that for you!"

She was on the brink of tears but decided not to be a whining baby. "See? I dreamed about you before I even met you! And then I saw you in the hospital after Will's fall and I felt like I knew you. And I prayed so hard that you'd feel the same way about me one day, and here it is."

He held her close and whispered in her ear, "I love you, Annie Louise. I love you with all my heart. Will you marry me?"

She didn't answer right away because she couldn't talk. She cried uncontrollably and Jonathan did his best to console her. He held her tightly and stroked her back, which seemed to help a little. He whispered sweet words in her ear and they had somewhat of a calming effect because she sat up and reached for her handkerchief on the end table. She wiped her eyes and blew her nose. Finally, she was able to talk.

Jonathan was watching her through his own wet eyes and

admiring her strength. He hated that she hurt so much inside. He wanted to wave some magic wand over her body and make all the awful memories of abuse that she suffered at the hands of the Barton family go away for good, but he knew they never would really leave her mind. All he could do was love her, and that was the easy part.

"I think I just needed a good cry," Annie said. "There's something about a cry that's cleansing. It has been just exhausting seeing Dub in the courtroom and everyone thinking he's guilty of murder. And then Verneice has to show up and stir the pot. I know it's just a matter of time before Mama D is on the stand, and it's like my past is before me once again."

Jonathan sat up in bed and reached for her to come into his arms. She rose slightly from the covers and he embraced her small frame. She nestled her head on his bare chest and buried her nose in his chest hair that hinted of British Sterling cologne. His chin was touching the top of her head and he talked softly above her ear. She fell limp in his arms listening to his soothing voice and all the wonderful well-pronounced words through his lips. It was the closest thing to heaven that she'd ever felt. She closed her eyes and could feel his heart beating in her ear. He pulled her chin up to his mouth and kissed her gently on the lips.

"You are the most beautiful woman in the world," he said softly between kisses. "And I am the luckiest man alive."

She reached over and turned out the light, but they didn't get to sleep until two hours later.

And she said 'yes,' *again,* to his proposal of marriage.

36
THE TRIAL,
DAY 3

The trial's slow pace had everyone concerned. Bets were being placed on the date it would end. By its third day, only two witnesses had come forth to testify – three if you count Verneice Stokes. Now it was Day 3. Who would be sitting in that hot seat today?

"The prosecution calls Sheriff Larry Haynes to the stand."

The sheriff walked up without his Stetson on his head and placed his left hand on the Bible and raised his right hand to be sworn in. He sat down in the witness seat and the D.A. pounced on him.

"Sheriff Haynes, please share with the court your findings regarding the human bodies found in the hog pen on Dub

Thomas' farm, and the human bones discovered under the garage of Tinker's Tow & Garage."

The sheriff was nervous with so many eyes on him. He was not used to a large audience listening to him at the same time. He cleared his throat and began talking about his investigation.

"Well, I was contacted by two homicide investigators and a forensic pathologist from Memphis who came to Cook with the results from the bones found under the garage," he said. "The pathologist determined that the death of the victim occurred about 15 to 20 years ago, and they wanted me to investigate who owned Tinker's Tow & Garage, who drove the two vehicles, particularly the wrecker, and to find a logbook that would show when the wrecker went out to pick someone up, where that someone was picked up and where that person was taken."

"I see," said the D.A. "I just don't understand why the Memphis police were investigating the bones. Why wouldn't it have been the Herndon police? Cook is in Herndon County, correct?"

"Yessir, but I don't know why," said the sheriff. "I think, but I'm not sure, that the company that was installing the tornado shelter for Mrs. Annie Barton is headquartered out of Memphis and they reported their findings to their corporation's city. That's just a guess, sir. I didn't question any of the authorities."

"Okay, sheriff, let's move on. What did you find out from the investigation on your end?"

"Well, I found out that the logbook is nowhere to be found," he said.

"And why is this logbook so important?" the D.A. asked.

"Because it would say exactly who was driving the wrecker on any particular night, what kind of call came in, the time of that call, who was picked up and where that person or persons was taken and what that person or person's was driving. That's why."

"And who did you ask about that logbook?"

The sheriff's sweat was running down his forehead into his eyes and he brushed his brow with his sleeve. "The investigators wanted to know if there were any residents of Cook that were reported missing from 1948 until 1953," he said. "I didn't take my job as sheriff until 1955, so I couldn't answer that. All I had were files that were not kept up-to-date."

The D.A. started walking around the courtroom with a pensive look on his face. The sheriff waited patiently for the next question, but the D.A. just kept looking up and around and down and back up. Then he decided to speak. "Please tell the court who you talked to and why."

The sheriff asked for a drink of water and the bailiff brought him a glass. He gulped it down and then wiped his forehead again and looked into the eyes of the D.A.

"Well, sir," the sheriff said, "I started with the widow of the owner of Tinker's Tow & Garage. Her name is Dorthea Barton, but people call her Mama D. She was married to the founder and owner, Minner Brown, but he died in 1940. So I asked Mama D who the drivers were around 1948 through 1953. I knew Dub was just a kid when he started driving the wrecker, like 14 thereabouts, so I figured he was driving from 1945 and on. But now that Mis' Verneice said he's younger than that, 1948 would have been his first year and he still could have been driving, I guess. But that would mean that he was really just 10 years old. Could that be? This is just so confusing."

The D.A. seemed confused, too. "So, sheriff, who else did you discover was also a driver?"

"Well, there was Minner Brown's uncle, James. And Minner's best friend, Jack Barton. And Minner's widow, Dorthea, could also drive the wrecker, if she had to."

"Did Mrs. Dorthea Barton cooperate with your questioning?"

"No, sir, she did not. She had just gotten out of prison and was holed up at a friend's house up in the hills, but she wouldn't talk to me about anything. She was very rude and bitter. You'd have to bring her to court to get anything out of her."

"Thank you, sheriff. No further questions," said the D.A., and he walked back to his seat.

Walt got up slowly, took off his reading glasses, and walked toward the sheriff. You could hear a pin drop in the courtroom.

"Sheriff Haynes," he said. "May I call you sheriff?"

"Yessir," the sheriff replied.

"Let's take a step back to the conversation you had with

the homicide investigators and the pathologist who visited you regarding the bones found under the diner."

"Okay," the sheriff said.

"Did they show you a report of any kind that indicated how they knew the body was female and that the bones were 15-20 years old?"

"No sir. They just told me in person."

Walt looked around the room at the jury and the spectators in their seats. They were mesmerized by this guy, and couldn't wait to hear what was going through his mind.

"I don't know how *you all* do business here in Tennessee, but in my great state of Illinois, we have pathology experts who fill out forensic reports on bodies. And are you telling me and this court that you never saw one of those reports? That all you got was a conversation between you and three other officials from Memphis?"

"Yessir," the sheriff said.

Walt felt like he had stepped back in time. He looked at the judge and said, "Your Honor, I have no more questions for this witness. May the prosecutor and I approach the bench?"

The judge told the sheriff he could step down and then he asked D.A. Moody and Walt to approach the bench.

"Your Honor," said Walt, "I would like to call the Memphis forensic pathologist to the stand to give us the official report of the body that was found under the diner's garage. He has been out of the country but has just arrived to testify, but he is not on the official list of witnesses."

"Mr. Moody, are you okay with that?" the judge asked.

"Yes, sir," the D.A. replied. "Get him sworn in. I'm anxious to know myself how they came up with those years."

The two lawyers walked back to their seats. Walt called the next witness.

"The defense calls Doctor Frank Myers to the stand."

Dr. Myers rose and walked to the bailiff to be sworn in before his testimony and then sat down in the witness chair.

"Doctor Myers, please state your name and occupation for the court," asked Walt.

"Doctor Frank Myers, forensic pathologist."

"Thank you, sir. Who is your employer?"

"I work for a medical school in Memphis," the doctor replied.

"And how did you come to work for the Memphis police with their investigation involving the bones found in Cook?"

"I work for them from time to time," he said. "I am always happy to help in any way I can."

"Will you please tell the court how you came up with the

years 15 to 20 when determining the age of the bones found behind the diner's garage? And also, sir, how do you know they are female?"

Everyone in the courtroom was interested in the doctor's testimony.

"Well, sir, there are several ways to tell the age of bones. One is by color. The older the bone the darker they are. The color of the bones found under the diner were consistent to 15-20 years of being buried. And we knew they were female because of the pelvis."

"The pelvis?" asked Walt. "Please explain."

The doctor continued. "Females have distinct pelvic features that are characteristic of childbearing. Men do not have those features. And men's bones are larger. Those were definitely female, a young female."

"Were you also the doctor who evaluated the human bones that were found in Dub Thomas' hog pen?"

"Yes, I was. Those, too, were female. But unlike the bones found under the garage in soft earth and protected from the weather, the bones in the hog pen were contaminated with animal blood, feces, rotting food, mud and other unidentifiable liquid. It was difficult to determine age, but they were definitely female. And there were three of them."

Those in the courtroom let out a gasp in unison.

"Three of them, sir?" Walt asked.

"Yes, three young women. It was just the most contaminated crime scene I have ever witnessed. I could not tell you their exact age, but we found three female pelvises and teeth that had come from three separate mouths."

Another gasp from the courtroom.

"Teeth?" Walt asked. "Did you find teeth under the diner's garage?"

"Yes, we did find teeth there. And the victim's dentist identified them for us."

"How did you know what dentist to contact?" asked Walt.

"Well, sir, we got lucky with that one. Unbeknownst to the person who took that young girl's life, two clues to her identity were buried with her. One was a necklace and the other was her teeth. When the parents recognized the necklace that was featured in the local newspaper, we notified the deceased's dentist and he verified that they were her teeth."

"Were those the only clues that were found with the victim that was under the diner's garage?" Walt asked.

"No sir," the doctor said. "There was also a pin with the Masonic Lodge insignia."

"Interesting," said Walt. "Thank you, sir, for coming forth today."

"My pleasure," said the doctor.

"Mr. Moody?" the judge asked.

"No questions, your Honor," said the D.A.

The judge struck his bench with the gavel. "Court is dismissed until one o'clock."

Everyone got up to leave and police had to guard Walt from all the ladies who wanted to speak to him. Finally, he was free to eat lunch and he caught up with Annie and Jonathan who were waiting for him outside.

"Good work in there, Walt," said Jonathan.

"Yeah, Walt, you sure can hold the attention of an audience," said Annie.

Walt lit a cigarette and took a long puff. "Yeah, but something's not right. I don't know what it is, but I am going to find out. C'mon, let's go get some lunch. All this talk about blood and guts has me craving food."

Jonathan and Annie just stared at him.

Walt started laughing and patting Jonathan's back. "I'm just kidding! It was a joke! But I am serious when I say that I need someone to get their hands on a list of all the members of the Masonic Lodge that are from Cook, Tennessee. That right there might point the finger at the murderer."

37

THE LOCKED BOX

After Annie, Jonathan and Walt ate lunch, they returned to the courtroom to listen to a few more witnesses before the judge adjourned for the day. The witnesses had been boring, not at all like the drama that previous witnesses had created.

It was exhausting and depressing hearing about dead bodies and how they were identified. The whole courtroom scenario was not Annie's cup of tea, and her fears of a bad outcome for Dub were mounting. All afternoon she stared at the back of his bald head. Every once in a while he would glance in her direction and look at her briefly before turning back around.

She was so happy now to be in her home and out of the courtroom. With Jonathan at his place in Lake Wheatley, she could spend quality time with her children. Becky had a project to complete for the following day at school and all of them practically ransacked the house looking for items to glue on her poster that was titled: "Five Things I Cannot Live Without."

Becky found a picture from Christmas of her entire family – Dwayne, Will, Noble, Boone, Buddy, her Mama and her future Daddy, Dr. Shea – and glued it on first. Then she taped her rabbit's foot, a skate key, her change purse and favorite necklace with a crucifix. After examining the five items, she decided against using the necklace because it had to be taped on the poster board and she was afraid it would get loose and fall off. So off she went in pursuit of something else. The boys gave up on her project and went outside to play. While looking for the last item for her project, Becky found a box with a lock on it under her mother's bed. She brought it out to the kitchen to show her.

"Mama, what's in this box?"

Annie turned around from the sink and saw the box and let out a squeal of happiness. "Oh, praise the Lord!" she cried. "You found my box! I have looked all over for it and couldn't remember where I put it! Thank you, baby girl!"

Becky was curious about its contents. "What's in it, Mama?"

"I don't know, hon," said Annie. "But it came from the creek."

"Like the book, Mama?" Becky asked.

261

"Yeah, baby, like the book. But I don't know how to get this dang lock off."

Becky had a big grin on her face. "I know who can get it off, Mama!"

"Who?" Annie asked.

"Buddy. He can open anything."

"Well, okay then!" said Annie. "Let's get him over here!"

Annie was reluctant to call Clyde's store where Buddy was working because Clyde would answer the phone and she had not talked to him since the whole Verneice spectacle in court. He had lied to her about Dub's upbringing and she just didn't want to go through that whole mess right now.

"How about you call Mr. Clyde, Becky?"

"Okay, Mama!"

Buddy was at Annie's house in five minutes. That was how long it took him to take off his green apron, clock out, and run to their front door. He brought his clippers with him and the lock was off in a matter of minutes.

Becky got Buddy a glass of lemonade and sat on his lap while Annie opened the box that was sitting open on the kitchen table. The whole room smelled like cigarettes when the lid was lifted, and it was full of a lot of different items. Annie began to take things out one at a time. A logbook was on top, and underneath it was a lot of photographs of young girls alone and girls with their

262

families. At the bottom was some jewelry.

"Who does it belong to, Mama? Who are those people?" asked Becky.

Heat was rising up Annie's neck and onto her ears and face. Feeling faint and about to puke, Annie sat down in the kitchen chair and took in some deep breaths. Becky and Buddy were confused.

"What, Mama? What's wrong?" asked Becky.

"It's just grown-up business, honey," she replied. "I want you and Buddy to go into the living room and turn on the TV. I think we have something here in this box that is very important and I need to call the sheriff."

Buddy did as his sister requested and Annie called Sheriff Haynes. He was at her house 15 minutes later. They went out into the back yard and sat at the picnic table under the tree. It was a beautiful March evening and still bright outside, but she felt it was all going to hell now with this discovery.

The sheriff's eyes opened wide when he saw the logbook. He turned each page and sighed. He looked at all the photographs and smiled. "We got the sonofabitch," he said.

Annie didn't ask who that sonofabitch was because she knew he couldn't tell her. He looked her in the face with a grateful smile. "Thank you, Annie, for calling me and letting me know about this important box. You know I can't share any information with you, but I need to get in my car now and drive to Memphis and talk to the detectives there. I just need to know one thing from you."

"Of course," said Annie. "Ask away."

"Where and when did you find this box, and where has it been all this time?"

"Oh, is that all? I can answer that," she giggled. "I found the box on my creek's bank right after the tornado. I couldn't open the lock, so I put it under the bed to deal with later. But then I forgot where I put it. Becky found it today when she was looking for something to use on her poster board for school."

"How did you open it?" the sheriff asked.

"I didn't," she replied. "We called Buddy and he opened it for us."

"Did you remove any of the items?"

"Yessir, we looked at everything briefly before I realized what we were looking at," Annie said.

"You all may be called to testify in court about this, I think," said the sheriff.

"Okay, we can do that," replied Annie.

"One last thing, Annie, and then I have to go," said the sheriff. "You can't tell anyone about what you saw in the box. If you do, that person or persons becomes liable and will have to appear in court. Understood?"

All of a sudden the box took on a monster-under-the-bed feeling inside her body. "Yessir, I understand."

He walked to his vehicle and drove away. Annie went inside to tell Buddy and Becky that they could not tell anyone about the box or they could go to jail. Becky started crying.

"But we didn't do anything wrong, Mama," she sobbed.

Annie held her precious baby girl and caressed her hair. "I know, honey. You did everything right and let me tell you why, okay?"

Buddy was sitting on the couch listening to Annie's every word. He wanted to crawl up into her arms, too. "You look like our Mama," he said to her tenderly.

Annie made a sad face and motioned for him to come to her side. She sat in the rocker with Becky in her lap and her right arm around Buddy who was sitting on the floor next to her.

"Now, listen to me, Becky," Annie said. "You and Buddy are heroes."

Becky was sucking on her first two fingers of her right hand, just like Annie used to do as a child. She pulled them out of her mouth and said, "Like Superman, Mama?"

"Yes, kinda like Superman. He always helped people and didn't want anyone to know it was him, remember?"

Becky and Buddy both nodded their heads.

"Okay, so what happened here today is this . . . Becky found a box that contains information that may be used in a court of law. And Buddy helped to open it, so he is involved now, too. And I went through the contents in front of you and now we are all in this together."

"So some bad guy is going to go to jail?" Buddy asked.

"I'm not sure, Buddy. But no one can know that you looked in that box. Understood?"

"Yes, ma'am," he replied.

"Yes, Mama, I won't tell nobody," said Becky.

"That means you can't tell Will and Dwayne, either. Or your other uncles, Noble and Boone, and anyone else you know, understood?"

They both nodded 'yes.'

"Okay, so how about we go up to the diner and eat some of Henry's cooking?"

Becky ran to the bathroom to wash her hands and returned with a towel tied around her neck and trailing down her backside.

"Do you like my cape, Mama?" she asked, smiling like a little angel.

Annie started laughing. "Yes, sweet girl, I do."

They walked out the front door and found Will and

Dewayne playing marbles near the porch. They laughed at Becky wearing the towel and pulled it off her back and ran down the road with it. She started running after them and then stopped and turned toward her mother and Buddy.

"Super people don't need capes, do they, Mama?" she asked.

"No, hon," Annie replied. "They just need to have a good heart, like you. If they did have capes, everyone would know who they are and expect them to do certain things for them. And how are they supposed to help the world when everyone knows what they're up to?"

"It's our secret," Becky said.

"And our mission," said Buddy, scooping up his little niece and hugging her neck.

"I love you, Buddy," she said sweetly.

"I love you more, Becky. Remember how I hid my hands?"

"Yeah," she said quietly.

"You made me strong," he said, kissing her on her cheek.

Annie put her arms around both of them and they continued their walk to the diner.

38
DUB'S PITY PARTY

Dub sat on a bunk in his jail cell and watched a roach scurry across the floor and through the bars into the free world. He wished he had a simple way out like that, but the tables were not turning in his favor.

His stomach began to ache while thinking about what life would be like behind bars – eating slop for breakfast, lunch and dinner, doing hard laborious jobs and fighting off the freaky perverted inmates who wanted to penetrate his orifices. But then he smiled and looked up at the ceiling where he knew God was watching down on him and said, "Well, Lord, it really isn't much different than when I lived with my so-called parents and so-called siblings now, is it?"

Everything in his life thus far had been one lie after another, except for those spent with Annie. She was the only joy he could muster up in his fried brain. She was real and her feelings were genuine. Yeah, he knew she was engaged to marry the doctor, but thoughts of being with her made his days behind bars more tolerable. She was his true constant friend, but he also knew she loved him like no one else ever had. Maybe not as a mate, but more than a brother. He wasn't sure where he fit in, but it felt like a good fit for them right now.

He smiled when he recalled the day she jumped into his truck and hugged his neck when he returned to Cook after a short time away. She was exciting to be around and he loved her energy. The children brought him so much joy and he imagined marrying her and living with her and the children the rest of his life.

And just when he was feeling pretty good about himself while thinking of Annie, his mind switched gears back to the dark days and he began riding that nasty oil slick again.

He remembered trying hard as a young boy to fit in with his family, but they just never connected. As he and the older children aged, they grew even more apart. Starving for love and affection, he threw himself into his work to feel good about himself, working long hours for Minner Brown and helping people get their cars out of ditches, and later, as he grew older, he'd run Cook's citizens back and forth to the hospital in Herndon. The community of Cook became his family of choice, and Annie was the icing on the cake.

He knew he was different from his family members, too. They all had dark hair and his was a dirty blond. They liked to read and drink hot tea. He liked to play cards and drink beer. But he never imaged his mother as Verneice. His whole body shook with repulsion when he recalled his thoughts as a teen about how hot Verneice was, even imagining what she was like in bed. He almost vomited.

But Clyde as his dad? Now that was the ultimate shocker, but he liked that a lot. "What a great guy Clyde is," he thought. "And I've got his genes pumping in my body. No wonder I like baseball!" he laughed.

His mind went haywire thinking about all the times he talked to Clyde and that Clyde probably knew that he was his son. And then Maydell Stokes' image popped into his head. He grabbed the pillow from the cot and buried his head in it while thinking about that wonderful woman who was his grandmother and he didn't even know it.

"But *she* did," he whispered aloud. "*She did!*"

He recalled getting a hug from her every time they parted ways. She always asked how he was doing and if he needed any money. His eyes filled with tears for Maydell, who he will never get to talk to ever again thanks to Mama D throwing an iron across the room that was meant for Verneice, but hit Maydell in the head instead.

And now he was the one that was staring at a jail sentence and maybe death.

His pity party was suddenly interrupted by a guard's voice hollering, "Thomas, you've got a visitor. Five minutes. That's all you got."

Dub sat up in the bunk and wiped his eyes with the blanket. He straightened his clothes and stood up to see Walt's huge torso approach his cell door. He was smiling from ear to ear.

"Hello, Mr. Thomas," Walt said.

Dub nodded.

Walt turned toward the guard and asked if he could speak to his client alone. The guard shot him a stupid smirk and reluctantly said, "Okay, buddy, but you got five minutes. You can't jest show up and expect us to jump through hoops."

Anger slowly rose from Walt's chest to his face. "I am not asking you to do that, sir," said Walt. "First of all, I am not your buddy, understood? And secondly, and most importantly, I have crucial business to discuss with my client. The last I read and heard, there is no limit to my visits or any time restraints. Your job is to process him, feed him, and escort him from the jail cell to the courtroom. Perhaps it is you, sir, who is asking me to jump through hoops in order to accommodate your schedule. You can stand here with me or wait at the end of the hall or take a shit in the crapper. I really don't care. I'm not asking for a sit-down. I am just going to talk to him through the bars, understood?"

The police officer looked more pissed off than apologetic and just walked away without answering Walt. Dub was excited witnessing the power of Walter J. Briscoe. *Why couldn't he have been my dad?* he thought to himself.

"Hey, man, how are you doing?" asked Walt. "It has been one surprise after another for you, eh?"

271

"Yessir, it has," answered Dub.

"Are they treating you okay?"

"Yessir."

"Well, they are going to be treating you like you own the town and are the only one who can determine if they go to Heaven or Hell, know what I mean?" asked Walt.

Dub's heart started thumping loudly in his chest. "What are you saying, Walt? I'm getting outta here? What's going on? Did someone confess?"

"Now, now, one thing at a time, Dub," Walt said. "Just let me say that evidence has literally been uncovered that will exonerate you. We've got one more day in court to bring it to the judge and jury and we expect that you will be released as a free man."

Dub sat down on his cot and put his head in his hands and sobbed quietly. He looked up at Walt through tearful eyes and asked, "Is that all you can tell me?"

"For now, yes, but tomorrow we will make it official for the court, the city, the newspaper and the world. You are not a killer, Dub. Guess I didn't have to tell you that. Just trust me, okay? Everything is going to be smelling like roses real soon. Get some rest and put on your Sunday best because tomorrow it's showtime!"

39
THE MELTDOWN

A loud pounding on Annie's front door woke her from a deep sleep just before daybreak on Friday morning.

"Who is it?" she asked.

"I am a representative from Walter J. Briscoe's office," he said.

She unlocked the door and saw a young, thin man about 21 years old. "Because you have not been released from the court, Mrs. Barton, Mr. Briscoe would like to remind you that you might be called to the stand as a witness again."

"Oh, okay, I will be available," she said. "I have been there every day."

"Thank you, ma'am," he said as he turned to leave.

Annie shut the door and walked toward the kitchen to put the percolator on the stove. She thought about her telephone conversation with Walt the previous day when they discussed her testimony. He told her to be truthful in court about how she found the locked box and to answer any other questions truthfully or to the best of her recollection. When they hung up, she placed a call to Lindy Sue's house and asked her to spend the night so that Lindy and the children could get dressed together and walk to the diner for breakfast before school.

After getting her caffeine fix, Annie woke everyone up and helped them get dressed before she had to leave. When she turned onto the tarred road, she saw a line of people standing on the front porch of Clyde's store. She rolled down the window of her truck and asked Lem Smithers what was going on. He was holding a newspaper that Harlan and Cleo had just delivered. He held it up so she could see the front-page headline and photo: NEW EVIDENCE IN THOMAS TRIAL. The accompanying photo showed Dub in jail clothes walking back to his cell with his head down, wearing handcuffs and leg irons. The sumdeck to the story read: "Jury to hear testimony today that could crack case wide open."

Annie's heart was beating fast and her eyes were teary. Her first instinct was that someone within the court system leaked information to the press about the locked box. She stepped on the accelerator and reached Herndon in record time. Lines were forming outside the building and it was difficult to find a parking spot, making her entrance much later than planned. She ran as fast as she could to the courthouse and reached it before the doors were locked shut. Panting and out of breath, she stood for the longest time until she could creep over to sit down.

Walt saw her come in and he leaned over to whisper something into Dub's ear, probably that she had finally arrived and that all was going to be okay. It wasn't long before she heard her name called to testify. The judge spoke first.

"I must remind you, Mrs. Barton, that you are still under oath," he said.

"Yessir," she replied.

"Please be seated."

Walt slowly rose from his seat and then pushed his chair back under the table. He walked toward Annie and she smiled.

"Mrs. Barton, what can you tell us about the tin box you gave to Sheriff Haynes?"

"Well, I found it on the creek bank behind my house after the tornado went through. I couldn't open it because it had a padlock on it. I washed the dirt off of it and put it under my bed and forgot all about it until the other day when my daughter found it and brought it to me."

"And what did you do then?" Walt asked.

"I tried to open it and couldn't, so my daughter said that her Uncle Buddy was good at opening things, so she called him at Clyde's store where he works. Buddy came right away and opened it with some kind of gadget, I'm not sure what it's called."

"When you opened it, who else saw the contents?" he asked.

Annie paused for a moment. Should she lie and say no one? Or tell the truth? *Walt said to tell the truth.*

"My six-year-old daughter, Becky, my brother, Buddy, and me," Annie said.

"Did you put everything back inside the box before you called the sheriff or did you or your daughter or brother keep any of the items?"

A tinge of resentment stung Annie. How could he think that she would keep any of that? "No sir, I did not keep any of it," she said coldly. "I realized it might be something really important pertaining to the trial because I kept hearing in court about a logbook missing and young girls missing and inside that box was all of that. So I put everything back the way it was and called Sheriff Haynes."

"Very good, Mrs. Barton. I would like for you to look at the contents again and verify that these are the contents that were inside the box," Walt said.

Annie said, "Okay."

Walt walked over to a large bulletin board on wheels that was covered with a white sheet. He picked up the bottom right corner of the sheet and tossed the fabric over the top of the bulletin board, revealing several 8" x 10" photographs of items from inside the metal box, including photos of young women.

Everyone in the courtroom was in awe of the faces and images that were visible. Pages of the logbook were also on display, as well as photos of jewelry and personal items.

"Do these appear to be the images that you saw in the box, Mrs. Barton?" Walt asked.

"Yes," Annie said softly.

"Thank you, ma'am, that will be all."

The prosecutor said he had no comments. The judge dismissed Annie.

Walt called Annie's Aunt Myrtle to the stand. She had been crying and blew her nose before walking up to be sworn in. Annie knew why she was there. It was her daughter's necklace that was found under the diner's garage alongside her bones. Aunt Myrtle confirmed that Exhibit 18 belonged to her daughter, Lurleen. She also provided the dates that Lurleen went missing.

There wasn't a dry eye in the courtroom for the next hour. Three other mothers were called to testify and identify that their missing daughters' photos were among those found in the metal box and on display on the courtroom's bulletin board.

The judge called a recess for lunch, and everyone was relieved to get outside and breathe in some fresh air.

But after lunch, Walt was back at it again. First up in the hot seat was Mama D.

"The defense calls Dorthea Barton to the stand," said

Walt.

Mama D waddled her way to the front of the courtroom to get sworn in. Her overweight body looked like a stuffed lobster in a tight red dress with gift-shop baubles around her throat and mid-section. She was sworn in and ready to talk.

"Mrs. Barton, I'm putting my trust in you today that you have a pretty good memory of the past and will be able to help the court."

"Yessir, I do have a pretty good memory all right."

"Well, that's all fine and dandy," Walt said, almost sarcastically, but Mama D took it as a compliment.

"Jest ask away," she said.

"Very good. I would appreciate it if you could answer some pretty easy questions for the jury, just to acquaint themselves with you. Would you be agreeable to that?"

"Yessir, I ain't got nuthin' to hide."

"Well, okay, then. Please tell the court of your relationship with Jack Barton."

Mama D let out a hearty laugh. "Why, that ol' buzzard was my second husband. Guess he got tired of waitin' for me while I was in the pen, cuz he done hung himself b'fore I got out."

The courtroom was silent. People were stunned by Mama D's lack of sensitivity.

"I'm so sorry to hear that, Mrs. Barton," said Walt. "And Mr. Minner Brown? How was he related to you?"

Mama D got choked up and had difficulty talking. The bailiff brought her a glass of water. "Minner wuz the love of my life. We had a son, who is now dead. Hell, they're all dead – Jack, Minner, Robert. But that bitch Annie is still alive …"

"Order! Order!" the judge ruled with his gavel. "There will be no name-calling in my courtroom using defamatory words like that. The jury will disregard that last sentence of Mrs. Barton's."

Walt cleared his throat and continued. "What was the relationship between Jack Barton and Minner Brown?"

"They wuz good friends b'fore Minner died. Jack helped Minner with the bizness, drivin' the wrecker and later the ambulance. They wuz like brothers."

"And after Minner Brown's death, you married Jack Barton?"

"Yep," said Mama D.

"Was he still working for Tinker's Tow & Garage?"

"Yeah, he still drove, even though we sold it to Minner's Uncle James."

"Who else drove?" asked Walt.

"Dub, of course. He was just a youngin' when he started, probably 14 or so."

"What did Dub drive?" Walt ask.

"Mostly the wrecker, but he weren't allowed to drive it outside of Cook. Only Jack could take those calls."

Walt scratched his head and looked over at the jury. They were mesmerized by him and followed his every move. He knew he had them under his spell, and decided to ask just one more question.

"Mrs. Barton, to the best of your recollection, when was Dub Thomas allowed to drive the wrecker and take calls outside of the jurisdiction of Cook?"

Mama D thought for a second before answering. "I don't rightly know the exact date, but it was prob'ly 'bout 1955."

Walt smiled so big you could see his gums. "Mrs. Barton, in an earlier testimony by Sheriff Haynes, he said that Dub was driving the wrecker in 1948. Do you have anything to add to that?"

"Whut? That ol' fart didn't ev'n live in Cook 'till '55. Whut the hell does he know 'bout anything? In 1948, Dub wuz jest a boy, for God's sake. We'd nev'r ev'r let nobody drive that young! That kid hung 'round the shop and warshed the vehicles, swobbed the floors, ran errands and did all kinds of shit for us. He was always at Tinker's and we had to tell 'em to go home a lot. He didn't start drivin' until he wuz 14, and nev'r, ev'r out of Cook 'til 'bout '55."

"So, if Dub wasn't driving outside of Cook, who was?"

Mama D rolled her eyes. "It was either Jack or James, but mostly Jack, cuz James was a sick man who couldn't lift a five-pound bag, know whut I mean? He wuz a weakling of a man."

Walt was in a groove and loved every minute of it. "Mrs. Barton, were you aware that the forensic pathologist in Memphis ruled that Lurleen Smith had been buried under the diner's garage for about 15 to 20 years?"

"No, sir, I wuz not aware of that," she said.

"You know what that means, don't you?" Walt asked.

Mama D paused for a few seconds and said, "No, whut, Mr. Hotshot?"

Walt chuckled and walked over to the jury box and looked right into the faces of the jurors. "It means, Mrs. Barton, that Dub Thomas could *not* have been the person who killed Miss Lurleen Smith or the three women whose remains were found in his farm's hog pen."

Walt turned around toward Mama D and continued. "It means that your husband, Mr. Jack Barton, was the only one driving the wrecker out of Cook during the time that those young women went missing."

The courtroom erupted with gasps and loud whispering. The judge had to calm everyone down.

"Order!" the judge yelled. "Order!"

Mama D was hotter than a wet hen. Flushed and out of breath, she managed to talk somehow. "How dare you say my Jack kilt those women! You ain't got no proof that he was anywheres near them! Y'all are all sons-of-bitches tryin' to pin somethin' on my dead husband. Y'all ain't got no proof!"

"But we do, Mrs. Barton," said Walt calmly, with a faint smile. "We have the logbook of his travels. During the time that Lurleen Smith went missing, your husband was called to an area where Miss Smith had been seen hitchhiking. He pulled over and she got up in the cab of his wrecker and he killed her. Maybe right away … or maybe after he had his way with her."

"Objection!" said the prosecution. "Your Honor, Mr. Briscoe is making up a scenario in his mind for the court and the witness. There's no proof to any of that."

Mama D smiled and stuck her tongue out at Walt. The courtroom erupted with laughter.

"Order! Order!" the judge yelled. Tranquility finally took over the courtroom as the judge contemplated the prosecutor's objection. You could hear a pin drop while he debated in his head if he should overrule or sustain.

And then suddenly he yelled, "Overruled!"

A few people started to clap and the judge slammed down the gavel three or four more times. "Order in the court," he yelled.

Walt smiled and continued his cross-examination.

"Mrs. Barton, there is proof that Lurleen Smith was on a highway hitchhiking and your husband was on that highway, too, at the same time and place. A witness saw her thumbing a ride, and there is also proof that the bones found under the garage of

Tinker's Tow & Garage have been identified as Miss Smith's, thanks to your husband's forgetfulness of leaving her necklace around her neck while in a hurry to bury her remains."

The courtroom started to moan.

"Objection!" shouted the prosecution. "Speculation."

"Objection overruled," said the judge. Please proceed, Mr. Briscoe."

"Thank you, your Honor," Walt said.

He walked over to the jurors and placed his hands on the railing of the wooden jury box that sequestered them from others in the room. He turned around and faced Mama D from afar. "Mrs. Barton, do you honestly think that someone other than your husband brought Miss Smith's body to Tinker's Tow & Garage and buried her in the ground there?"

Mama D put her head down and waved him off with her right hand.

The courtroom was so silent that Walt could hear his heart pounding in his chest. Everyone was clinging to his words like their own life depended on it. He was in his element. It was moments like these that made him crave the courtroom long after each case. And he wasn't done with Mama D just yet.

"And, Mrs. Barton," he said, "the other three female victims whose bones were found in the hog waller on Dub's farm, were all in one car when it began having difficulty, and all three women walked to a house nearby and called the nearest wrecker.

Their car had a flat tire, but that's not why they had to call a wrecker. The tire was flat, all right. But when they pulled over, the driver didn't see the ditch alongside the road and the car went over on its side. All of the night's events were written up in a detailed report in the logbook of Tinker's Tow & Garage, signed by your husband's hand."

Everyone wanted to clap, but knew it wasn't the right protocol for a courtroom. They did whisper loudly, sounding like the humming of a swarm of bees, and the judge had to throw down the gavel again. Everyone thought that Walt was done with the witness, but he had a few more things up his sleeve they didn't see coming.

"Are you done with me yet, Mr. High & Mighty?" Mama D asked.

Walt just flashed his pearly whites at her and calmly said, "Not just yet."

"Well, then, jest git to it. Bring it on!!!" she screamed.

The judge slammed his gavel down on the bench and called for order again. Walt apologized and continued with his cross-examination.

"Mrs. Barton, we also have evidence that puts you at the scene of one of the crimes," he said calmly.

"Oh, you do, do you? Like whut?" she asked, sarcastically.

Walt walked over to the evidence board and took down a white sheet of paper that was covering another one. "Your father's

Masonic Lodge cufflink, which you had made into a lapel pin."

There, on the bulletin board magnified at least 500 percent was a photo of the topside and backside of the cufflink/lapel pin that was found with Lurleen's body under the garage.

All the blood left Mama D's face and left her looking like a ghost with its mouth open.

"You know, Mrs. Barton? When I saw that pin in the evidence pool I kept trying to find the man it belonged to. I must have asked everyone in Cook if they had lost a Masonic Lodge pin, and I even took out an ad in the *Herndon Chronicle* but no one responded. And then I got lucky when I talked to the preacher, Pastor Russell. He said that Jack Barton pinned it to your dress's collar when you got married in the pastor's church because your father had just died and Mr. Barton couldn't afford a diamond ring. So, you had your father's cufflink made into a pin that you could wear every day for good luck. But I guess your luck just ran out."

Mama D started to cry, but no one felt sorry for her. A police officer walked over and asked her to stand up. She did, and then he asked her to put her hands behind her back, which he shackled. He led her down the steps of the witness stand and right passed Dub. She wiggled free from the officer and got right up in Dub's face and screamed, "You tell that Annie girl of yourn that I knowed Jack is Will's daddy. And I knowed all along that yore daddy was Clyde Tubbs."

The officer tried to pull her away but she stood firm, lashing out at Annie next, who was sitting next to the jury box.

"This is all your fault!" she yelled. "We took you in so Jack wouldn't go after them girls anymore. But you kept gettin' pregnant. You just done ruined it all. Yore a damn whore!"

Dub spit a projectile loogie in Mama D's face while three officers took her away.

Annie fainted. The bailiff propped her up in her seat while a few old ladies fanned her face. Suddenly, her eyes shot wide open when she inhaled Jonathan's cologne.

"Hey, sweet girl! That was some exit," he said with a big smile.

Annie just stared at him like she didn't even know who he was. About 15 seconds later, she realized she was not in a dream, and threw her arms around him, sobbing. Everyone scattered and left the young couple alone.

He grabbed each of her hands from around his neck and put them in front of his chest and stared deep into her eyes. "What happened, hon? What made you snap like that? You looked like you didn't even know me! I'm wondering if you are suffering from shock."

He pulled out a tiny flashlight and looked into each of her eyes to see the size of her pupils. Her face wrinkled up, signaling a crying spell that was about to surface.

"What?" he pleaded. "What is wrong?"

She leaned forward and whispered in his ear, "Daddy Jack is Will's father," she said softly. "Is being a sex addict and a serial killer hereditary? Because Becky might be his child, too."

40
PEACE, AT LAST

The whole town of Cook, Tennessee, came out for Dub's homecoming. Covered dishes filled the tops of about 30 picnic tables that were set up on his property, and the aroma from seven barbecue grills activated everyone's taste buds.

"Welcome Home" signs dotted the road leading to Dub's farm, and an anonymous citizen rented a limo to pick him up at the jail and bring him home to his farm. He thought Annie's kids might like to see what the inside of a limo looked like, so he invited them to ride along with him. There was even room for Annie and Jonathan.

"Y'all are my family," Dub said proudly when they climbed inside the huge vehicle.

Becky said the limo looked like it was part of a Disneyland ride she saw on TV, but they all agreed it felt like they were in a parade when they saw townspeople lining the road holding more signs and waving and clapping as the limo passed. Once they arrived and Dub climbed out of the car, his hunting dog, Duke, ran up to him and jumped into his arms, smothering his master's face with kisses and howling loudly.

Residents were overcome with emotion and crying with happiness at Dub's welcome home party, joyful that something good was finally happening for them in their beloved Cook. The trial served as a cleansing for a majority of townsfolk after suffering through a tremendous loss of human life caused by a killer tornado earlier in the year, and finding one of their beloved teacher's skeleton hanging onto a tree root in Pig Dog Creek six years earlier.

The evil caused by Mama D and Daddy Jack had been exposed and dealt with by a court of law, and the lies of Dub Thomas' biological parents were made public. But the coincidences surrounding Pig Dog Creek were up for debate. Many were happy with the thought that the creek had magical powers, while others were afraid and said they were threatening. About a quarter of those in attendance just washed their hands of any idea that a body of water could have any control on anyone's life, weather or phenomena of any kind, and that it was all "just plain hogwash." One person thought it could be invaders from Mars living there. Everyone had a good laugh over that.

A toast was made to a new beginning. When the day began to wind down, Dub asked Annie if she would join him for a walk because he had something to tell her that had been eating a hole in his gut. She found Jonathan and the kids throwing darts at a target nailed to the barn, and told him that she and Dub were going for a walk. Jonathan didn't seem to mind at all. He knew where her heart was.

Dub loved Annie more than any other human on earth, and he knew she loved him, too, but like a brother. She made that clear numerous times. But a life without Annie in it would be unbearable. He would take whatever she could give him. If that was just friendship, then that's better than nothing.

He held her hand as they walked behind his house to a secluded area by a small lake. They sat down on a bench that Dub had fashioned from a huge tree stump. Annie had never been on this side of his property, and it was breathtaking.

Dub grabbed her hand and put it to his mouth to kiss. She looked at him and smiled. "What do you have to tell me, Dub? Because it is making me very anxious, and I have had enough of that kind of feeling, you know?"

"Yes, I know," said Dub.

"Then spit it out now," she playfully demanded.

"Well . . . remember when everyone was looking for Becky?"

"Yes, I remember that day all too well. I still have nightmares about that. Why are you bringing that up? Because …"

Dub cut into her words. "I know," he said. You got really ticked off at me. You thought I wasn't lookin' hard enough to find her."

"Yes," she said, pulling her hand away from his. "You weren't. It was very disappointing. I still get a little angry thinking about that day and how you were acting."

A huge crane flew over the lake and they smiled at the sight of the beautiful bird and its wingspan. Dub reached out for her hand again. "Well, you are kinda right about me that day, but not totally."

"I'm confused, Dub," she confessed, already exhausted from the conversation's topic. She knew there wasn't anything that he could say that would make her forgive him for not being there when she needed him.

"I know! I know," he said. "Jest listen. I knew the tornado had followed the creek and I was having a panic attack wundering if it had torn up Martha Wilks' toolshed, so I snuck away from the search team to go see."

Annie stood up, put her hands on her hips and stared at the lake. She looked down at Dub and said sarcastically, "What the hell does that toolshed have to do with anything, Dub?"

Dub stood up, too, and looked into her face. Their eyes locked. "I hid something there that I found in the garage at Tinker's that was stuffed inside the wheel well of the wrecker. But the toolshed had been destroyed by the tornado."

Annie's mouth dropped. "What in the world did you hide there?"

Dub turned toward Annie and had tears in his eyes. He

could hardly speak.

"What is it, Dub? What was inside the wheel well?"

"It was the tin box you found on the creek bank with the padlock on it," he replied. "I didn't know what was in it until Walt showed me a picture of it. He said he got it from you."

"Whoa, now wait a minute," said Annie. "Are you saying the tornado tore Martha's toolshed to smithereens, but scooped up the tin box into its funnel and spit it out onto my creek bank? That's not near as bad as Maydell's bones being found there, but it's still pretty creepy, don't you think?"

"Yes," replied Dub, who was switching emotions from tears to rage thinking about the box's contents. "That old worthless-piece-of-shit Daddy Jack was hiding his trophies in the wheel well, probably pullin' the box out ev'r now and then and getting turned on while looking at the trinkets and photos he took from the women he raped and tortured. I even went to the reclaim center in Herndon to see if it had been turned in there."

Once again, Annie thought, the creek's mystical powers brought something to the surface. Last time it was a book that taught her to read and write, and then a human skeleton hanging on a tree root. This time it was a box of evidence. Annie felt queasy and had to sit down. Dub walked down to the water to wet his handkerchief to place on her forehead. When he walked back up, Jonathan was kneeling by her.

"Here," Dub said, handing Annie the wet cloth. "Put it on your forehead."

Jonathan touched her forehead first to see if she had fever. She didn't. Then he took her pulse, which was racing. "What has you so upset, hon?" he asked Annie.

Annie thought for a moment and then replied, "I think it's time we get married, Jonathan, and I have the perfect place picked out."

Jonathan looked at Dub and he shrugged his shoulders. "I dunno," he said.

"Okay," Jonathan said sweetly. "When and where?"

Annie choked back vomit that was coming up into her throat. "I want a Pig Dog Creek wedding, and I want it before this baby inside me starts showing."

The End

Made in the USA
Columbia, SC
05 January 2020